CHALKED AND LOADED

VANESSA GRAY BARTAL

DRY CREEK PRESS

PROLOGUE

Josie was not averse to shenanigans and fun times, especially on this, her eighteenth birthday. As if to prove how wild she was, she paused at the 7-11 and bought a massive Big Gulp. Blue, no less, guaranteed to turn her tongue an alarming color. Of course she only drank about five sips before remembering the potential cavitation from mouth plaque, but it was the principal of the thing. She could be crazy, as crazy as the next cardigan-wearing teenager.

A mass of humanity swarmed around her, an ordinary thing for rush hour on Friday. As usual everyone became a homogenous swarm of people, somehow indistinct. Despite having different skin colors, heights, weights, and clothes they all ended up as white noise in Josie's mind, a side effect of city life, she supposed.

Except one man.

Later she would think he wore a suit.

Much later she would say it was a hoodie and jeans.

Then she would revise again and say it was a suit because a hoodie and jeans would have been much less menacing.

In any case he stood in the middle of the sidewalk, an unmovable boulder in the river of humanity. People streamed around him, not even tossing him a look of annoyance, almost as if he didn't exist.

Josie saw him, however. She had been walking toward him, minding her own business, when she suddenly realized that, not only was he standing completely still, but he was staring. At her. His gaze, dark and intent, could be described as nothing less than creepy.

Josie came to a sudden halt, causing the person behind her to bump her back and mutter a curse.

"Sorry," she said, a tremulous murmur as the man stalked toward her. Should she run? Keep walking? Go the other way? What was the proper thing to do when a stranger approached with such intent?

In the end she did nothing but stand still, frozen like the proverbial deer.

"H-hello," she tried, tucking her hair behind her right ear in a nervous gesture. Maybe he was about to hit on her. Maybe when she turned eighteen some sort of alarm went off, telling older men she was now eligible and not illegal. Though boys her own age never hit on her, it was conceivably possible she attracted an older demographic, someone middle aged like this guy.

He stopped again, this time right in front of Josie, a few inches away, toes nearly touching. And then he spoke.

"Somehow, someday, someway, I am going to find you again. And I am going to kill you."

He took one step to the side and walked past her, disappearing into the crowd as if maybe he'd never been there at all.

CHAPTER 1

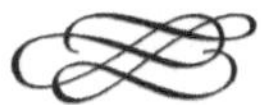

I f you weren't the guy who started the startup, then your reason to be there was probably born of desperation. That was the conclusion Tristan came to his second week at his job. And since he wasn't the person who started the company, that meant he was desperate, exactly like everyone else. The best thing he could say about his new job at this point was that he liked his boss. Ribs, the guy who started the private security firm, was the real deal, a former SEAL turned spy who got out of the game to be closer to his wife and kids. There was some backstory there, but Tristan didn't know and didn't care. All he needed to know was that the job paid real money and his boss wasn't a moron. So far, so good. It wasn't a lot of money, but it was enough to survive, with the promise of more as the company grew and took on new clients. Tristan would do his part to make certain they succeeded, not only because his work ethic was solid, but because this was the end of his road. If this job didn't work out, he'd have to play security guard at summer carnivals or something equally degrading. But as bad as that thought was, he didn't ponder leaving the security game because protecting people was all he knew. *Protect and serve.* What a joke.

Last week, his first week on the job, was orientation, acclimation, certification. Ribs wanted to make sure his gun permits and skills were all up to date, and Tristan liked that about him. He liked it even more when he used his contacts in the military to grant him access to a treasure trove of weapons to test. Last week had been like school, if school had ever been fun. This week the real work began, assuming they had work, which was a bit of an iffy prospect. People tended to go with the bigger, more established firms when life and death were on the line. *Patience,* Ribs had urged him. *The clients will come, I promise. I have a lot of contacts; they've promised to steer people my way.*

Tristan wondered if one of those contacts had been steered because when he looked up, Ribs stood in his office.

"Those are some silent feet," Tristan noted.

Ribs grinned at him. He was pretty smiley for a military guy, but Tristan supposed that was a good thing. The head of a company necessitated being good with people. If Tristan were in charge, they'd close up shop within a week.

"Got a client for you," Ribs said and sat without invitation. Since he technically owned all the furniture in their rented office space, it was probably his right.

Tristan's brows rose but he didn't say anything. It's not as if he made a game of not speaking, merely that he'd grown used to silence. Generally it put people on edge and they started to babble, garnering useful information for him.

"It's a *girl,*" Ribs added, brows wagging.

That got Tristan's interest. "Hollywood starlet?" He held up double crossed fingers. They'd both reached the conclusion that famous people would be their bread and butter. Acting as personal security for visiting celebrities was a dream come true, an easy gig that paid mind-boggling amounts.

Ribs shook his head.

"Politician?"

Ribs shook his head.

"Internet mogul?"

Ribs shook his head.

"Are you going to tell me?" Tristan asked, half annoyed, though he was more annoyed by his curiosity. He tried hard to be dead inside and resented anything that made him feel otherwise.

"I was enjoying seeing how many job possibilities you could come up with for a woman. Good news, the misogyny is low with you."

"Truly, I'm a feminist icon," Tristan said dryly, making Ribs laugh.

"Our new client is, are you ready for this?" He paused dramatically.

"You're losing your audience," Tristan told him.

Ribs tapped his fingers on the table, creating his own personal drumroll. Tristan must be a moron because it sort of worked, he could feel the suspense build as he waited for Ribs's revelation. Exactly how rich and famous was their new client? When Ribs finally uttered the words, Tristan had to shake his head and wiggle his ear to make certain his hearing was okay.

"What?"

"Kindergarten teacher," Ribs repeated, this time enunciating the words.

Tristan blinked at him. "Is she paying us in cookies?"

"That would be awesome, but no. Her grandfather died and left her some money. She's using that."

"What does she want us to do?" Tristan asked, still in the disbelieving tone.

Ribs grinned again. "You're going to have to hear it for yourself."

"Oh, boy," Tristan said, dropping his head to his hands. If it was enough to amuse a guy with Ribs's pedigree, it was bound to be a doozy.

Later he would think that "doozy" didn't begin to cover it.

⚷

*R*ibs told Tristan he wanted him to interview the new client at her place of business because, being a teacher, it was difficult for her to get away. Tristan had his suspicions about that. He would gladly have met her somewhere in the evening, after school was finished. Really he thought it amused Ribs to send him into an elementary school, like Arnold Schwarzenegger in *Kinder-*

garten Cop. Tristan wasn't as buff as Arnold, but almost, and equally unsmiling.

The client in question—Josie Davis—sat on a brightly colored rug sorting crayons into plastic bins. Tristan paused in the doorway, taking note of his first impressions. He'd been in the business long enough to know first impressions were usually garbage, but he always took them anyway.

Josie was petite with sandy blond hair tied neatly at her nape. Her face was tipped down, and he couldn't see it. She wore a plaid skirt and yellow sweater with—toads? Yes, toads knitted on the pockets— and black shoes that looked like ballet slippers. *Conservative and quirky,* was his first thought, but he supposed a kindergarten teacher would have to be. No one wanted to send little Johnny or Judy off to a teacher who looked like Courtney Love on a bender. Finished making his silent inspection, he cleared his throat.

"Blah!" Josie yelped, and tossed a handful of crayons into the air.

That was…that was kind of funny, he admitted. But he didn't let it show because he had mastered his expressions early in the game. "Miss Davis."

She squinted a frown up at him. "Are you telling me my name? Because I already know. What I don't know is yours."

She had a distinct and pedantic way of speaking that probably came in handy with five year olds but set his teeth on edge.

"My name," he pressed his palm to his chest, "is Tristan."

If she realized he was mocking her tone, she didn't let on. Her eyes scanned him up and down. "Are you freakishly big, or is it forced perspective because I'm on the ground?"

"There's no possible way to answer that question," he said.

"Would you mind sitting? I'd like to sort while we talk, but if I have to keep craning my neck at this angle I'm going to snap a vertebrae." She lowered her head and resumed her task. The rest of the room was in absolute chaos, toys asunder, a curtain half ripped off, two chairs toppled like there had been some sort of baby-sized brawl. Josie focused hard on the pile of crayons. The meticulous and methodical way she sorted them was almost defiant, as if she were purposely ignoring everything she couldn't control in favor of this tiny thing she could. Tristan sank slowly across from her, trying to remember the last time he sat on the floor. Maybe not since he was actually in kindergarten.

"How long have you been in private security?" Josie asked.

"Two weeks."

She whistled softly. "Clearly my money has bought me the best."

He knew she was joking, but he still bristled. "It did, in fact, but I have no idea why I'm here. Would you like to fill me in?" Watching her meticulously sort crayons, separating pink from dark pink and so on, it was impossible to believe she was in any danger. She sorted for a moment longer, and he got the impression that the sorting soothed her, especially because it would likely be undone within five minutes the next time kids touched the crayons. When she finally spoke, it was so soft he had to lean in to hear her.

"Someone is trying to kill me."

He tensed, frozen in sudden alarm, his first thought that he'd stumbled into a domestic situation. A husband, current or former, was the most likely suspect. "Who?"

"I don't know."

"How?"

"I don't know."

"When?"

"I don't know. And let me save you the trouble of asking where because I don't know that either."

He opened his mouth, closed it again, and studied her in fierce concentration. Clearly she was nuts, which was fine, lots of people were, but why was she paying them money to have that confirmed? "Do you have any other information?"

She finished sorting the crayons while Tristan stewed in silent misery. He didn't mind silence or waiting, but he liked it to be on his terms. Finally after she put all the crayons away and set the plastic bins on the shelf, she started to talk.

"On my eighteenth birthday, a guy stopped me on the street and told me he was going to kill me."

"Did he try to kill you then?"

"No, he said he'd come back for me, that he would find me and kill me at some unknown point in the future."

"Clearly he was insane," Tristan said. "No one does that, it doesn't happen. No one picks a girl at random and tells her that, unless all he's after is the thrill of telling her that. You probably made his day by being wide eyed and terrified."

"Wow, what a fresh take on a situation that's plagued me for ten years. I am so glad I paid my entire inheritance to hear you tell me what every police officer, family member, and friend has told me for a decade. Whew, what a relief. I can sleep now for, did I mention, the first time in ten years."

Her frowny face was pretty cute, but he was also annoyed. "If everyone has told you this, why don't you listen?"

She took a deep breath and let it out slowly through her teeth. "I'm going to explain this once, and that's it. If you're still obtuse after that, we'll end this arrangement and I'll take my money elsewhere."

He shifted, suddenly remembering he and Ribs desperately needed the money she was about to pay them. Crazy or not, he needed to take this case. The good news was that it would be a cake job because clearly no one was after her.

"Forget for a minute that you're eight feet tall, built like a tank, and have whatever training you have that makes you presumably good at this job. Pretend you're a small, helpless girl on her eighteenth birthday, optimistic over your future, when you realize a stranger is staring at you in the street. Not a random homeless person who is clearly mentally ill, but a well-dressed, put together man intent on talking to you, specifically to you. He stops you in the street and tells you that at some unknown point in your future, he will find you again, and he will kill you. And then he's gone, just like that. You try to blow it off, to tell yourself it was a random weirdo, intent on scaring a kid. But what if it wasn't? What if he actually knew who you were? What if he targeted you on purpose? What if he really does intend to kill you?

"But of course that's not rational, or so you repeatedly tell yourself as you try to go on with your life and live normally. You go to college as planned, you get a job, you have friends and a life. But do you ever stop worrying, wondering, looking over your shoulder, taking every possible precaution, just in case? The answer is no, you do not. But you want to, so desperately. You long to let go of the fear and anxiety that has held you captive for ten long years. You tell yourself it's okay to date, get married, have kids. That there's not some psycho stalking you who will take out the people you love most." She paused and took a deep breath. "That's all I want, to be able to let this go, to prove a negative, that no one is after me. To prove a positive, that I am safe. I want to, once and for all, put this completely behind me and move on, resolved that it was a random act. So if that's how you want to view it, by all means, please do. But don't discount the fear that has been my constant companion for ten years."

He was going to do the job anyway, he'd already established that he and his boss needed the cash. But he suddenly felt for her. It was small, but it was there. A heart that hadn't felt anything for a long time gave a whimpering lub and turned over because clearly this girl was struggling. It was likely that she struggled with a figment of her imagination, brought on by anxiety, but still. She was suffering. On the other hand he would gain nothing by giving her the upper hand and letting her know he sympathized, if only a little. So he gave her the blank stare, eyes dead and flat, while she stared at him with the teacher stare, stern and imposing. He glanced away and bit the inside of his cheek because it was a little cute, that stare. Like a guinea pig trying to be severe and commanding.

"If we do this, you need to know I'm going to delve into your life and take it apart, piece by piece. Down to the molecule. It's going to be intrusive, and if you have skeletons, prepare for me to see them. Because I will."

Now it was her turn to smile in amusement, which softened her face pleasantly. "I teach kindergarten and fall asleep by nine. The only skeletons in my closet are Halloween decorations."

"Okay." He started to unfold himself from his pretzel formation, but she put out a hand.

"Wait, I have one of those dramatic things to say, too. As you can probably imagine, my family wants me to let this go. They've been telling me to let it go the last ten years. To say they wouldn't be happy I'm spending my grandpa's money on this would be an understatement. They can't know."

"Were you there for the part when I said I'd be diving deep and tearing your life apart? They're going to know."

"They're going to know you're there and asking questions; they don't have to know you're from a security firm." She clasped her hands together and gave him a hopeful, pleading glance.

His lashes fluttered. It took a lot to shock him, but she managed. "Are you saying you want me to pretend to be your boyfriend?"

"Do you think we're filming an episode of *I Love Lucy*? Of course I don't want that, namely because it's crazy, and also because absolutely no one would buy it."

"Why not?" he blurted before he could stop himself.

"Because look at you, and look at me. I'm guessing I'm not your normal type, and I know for certain you're not mine. But everyone would buy us as friends."

"In your circle maybe," he said. He didn't exactly have female friends.

"Yes, in my circle. I have a lot of guy friends, always have. No one will think a thing of it if I add a new one."

"Fine, we'll pretend to be friends."

Now it was her lashes' turn to flutter. "We don't have to pretend. We could be actual friends."

She sounded a little soft, a little vulnerable. He should probably tread lightly.

"No," he said, then unfolded himself from the ground and left.

CHAPTER 2

Tristan thought there was nothing like sinking his teeth into an investigation to take his mind off his troubles. He didn't usually take a personal interest in the people portion of a case, that would be too intense. Instead he liked the puzzle aspect, enjoyed giving his brain a riddle to solve, the bigger, the better. The puzzle of Josie Davis might be the biggest one to date. That a woman so unremarkable and ordinary earnestly believed her life had been targeted would be laughable, if not for the extreme anxiety it had caused her. Tristan fully believed a man had stopped her on the street that day and threatened her life. He also fully believed the man had been either a crackpot or a psycho who did it for his own kicks and nothing more. Why? Because as long as he'd been in the field, he had never seen anyone show the sort of dedicated perseverance it would take to track a woman for a decade, to bide his time that long before making a move.

But he also realized he was going into the job with an unfair bias. He vowed to keep an open mind, but he also asked Ribs his opinion on the matter.

"Honestly? She seems like a sweet innocent who had a terrible fright as a kid, one that scarred her. If there's anything we can do to alleviate that fear and lay it to rest, then by all means let's do it."

There, they were on the same page. Josie had a real problem, and that problem was fear. They weren't taking money under false pretenses; they were performing a necessary service, like taking out a scary spider from the bathtub, only in this case the spider didn't exist. Tristan would prove it. To do that, he needed to go back to the beginning and gather the facts of her life. The event in question happened on her eighteenth birthday, adding another layer. It was feasible the day was significant, that the guy had a list of birthdays and sought out all the eighteen year olds that day. Who knew what made guys like that tick?

Random or targeted?

That seemed the most pertinent question to Tristan. If the threat had been random, they could discount it completely as crackpot nonsense. If it was targeted, they would need to discern if it had been targeted to Josie specifically or something about her. Maybe he said the same thing to all teenage girls that day, who knew?

"I'm going to set up a whisper network," he told Ribs during their briefing.

"Let me know if you need technical help; I have a consultant on standby," Ribs told him.

They couldn't yet afford a fulltime computer tech, which was a shame, since so much was done on the internet these days. Someday maybe they'd get there. For now everything would be done the old fashioned way—surveillance, interviews, and interrogation.

"I think I've got it, but I'll let you know," Tristan told him, his mind already running to all the sites he'd need to tap. He would pose a question on a few key social media pages and see where it landed. *My cousin had the weirdest experience about ten years ago. She was walking down the street one day when some guy approached and said he would find her again and kill her. Anyone ever heard of anything like that? She didn't know if it was a game or what. So crazy!*

He put some variation of that on four sites known for woolgathering speculation and conspiracy-laden theorization. If anyone had heard of similar stories, hopefully he'd get a hit in the next few days.

Secondary to that, he had to begin to delve into Josie's life. Ribs had already gathered all her pertinent data—date of birth, place of birth, social security number, and license number. Tristan sent requests to all the relevant locations: BMV, FBI, and anything else he could think of to make certain she wasn't lying to them. He didn't think she was, but it was always better to make certain. It would be awkward if their first case turned out to be a secret career criminal with a mile long history of incarcerations.

Third was the part he dreaded most: meeting her friends and family. Lucky for him (or maybe not?), she wasn't a transplant like much of DC. She had always lived local, and so did most of her friends and family. Tonight Tristan would meet them on the pretense of attending a family barbecue. *Kill me now,* he thought. *Small talk with strangers.* He would rather interrogate a hostile witness than shoot the breeze with Grandpa Joe any day of the week.

The plan was to pick Josie up and rehearse their story so they'd know the basics of their supposed friendship. She lived in a townhouse in a suburb on the north side of DC. It had a one-car garage, which was good for security. She could go from car to door without exposing herself on the walk between. Of course there could always be someone hiding inside the garage, able to obscure his nefarious deeds from the neighbors. But statistically it was safer than not.

Tristan wasn't certain if he was supposed to knock on her door. He didn't want to because it made it seem like a date, but he didn't have her number to text and she didn't come out when he pulled up. With a sigh he unbuckled, ascended the walk, and knocked.

She answered quickly, tossing him a succinct smile before closing and locking the door. "Hi, thanks for this."

"You know you're paying me, it's not actually a favor," he pointed out.

"Thank you for refuting my attempt at polite discourse while also making yourself sound like a gigolo," she said, tone significantly surlier.

He almost laughed, but caught himself in time, turning it into a cough instead.

"What should I know about you?" she asked as soon as she was buckled into his car. It was a no brainer that he'd drive; he couldn't abide riding in the passenger seat.

He placed his hand on her chair, anchoring himself as he looked behind him to reverse. The car slid onto the street. He faced forward. "Nothing."

She stared at his profile, waiting him out.

He kept his eyes forward, unperturbed.

"Okay, let me do a run through of our evening. This is Tristan, no last name. He enjoys awkward pauses and lifting weights. His inspiration is Gaston and he would like you to know it *is* possible to eat fifty eggs and be the size of a barge."

"I thought it was in bad taste to comment on people's size these days," he said.

"Not if it's something they've purposely worked toward. Like I have this friend who wears a waist shaper, and I tell her she looks like an hourglass, because I know it's what she's working toward. It's complimentary."

He flicked his eyes at her but otherwise didn't comment.

"Unless you were born like this and you've secretly been trying to unsuccessfully get scrawny, in which case I apologize, both to you and your mother because that must have been one hard labor."

He coughed again, scrunching his face to avoid giving way to a smile.

"Would you like a lozenge?" she offered.

He flicked a glance toward her again. "Do you actually have lozenges?"

"Teacher voice," she said, tapping her throat. "You try talking seven hours straight and see if you can survive without lozenges. My lozenge budget grew so enormous I began making my own."

This time he waited to look at her until they reached a stoplight because that required a longer gaze. "You make your own lozenges."

"You don't have to say it like that."

"Like what?"

"Like I have Charles Manson on speed dial because I have a lozenge hobby. It's not so weird."

He faced forward again but held out his hand, palm up. She placed her palm in it and gave it a shake. He sighed. "That was for a lozenge."

"You gave me a handshake for a lozenge? I would have given you one for free," she said.

"I was holding out my hand for a lozenge," he said through gritted teeth. It was taking all his focus to talk to her and stay on the road. He wasn't certain he would be able to describe this conversation to anyone after the fact, nor that he would ever want to. Lozenge hobby? Who was this person?

She dug in her purse and placed a little round disk in his hand. He popped it in his mouth, tipping his head at the unexpected heat.

"Ginger," he declared.

"I'm more of a blond," she said.

He sighed.

She poked his bicep. "That was a little jokey joke."

"A very little," he said and bit back a smile when she laughed.

"Do you have a girlfriend?"

He tossed her a look. She held up her hands in surrender. "I'm making conversation, not measuring you for tuxedos which, if I haven't mentioned, would be enormous. Like Kronk from *Emperor's New Groove,* a 66 long and a 31 waist."

"I literally have no idea what you're talking about," he said.

"Right, guys like you always have a secret Disney fetish. You probably have Cinderella stuffed in your closet. Are you a Brony?"

He choked again. She fished out another lozenge and held it out to him. "You need to get that cough looked at."

"It's a new development," he said, taking the lozenge. He pulled into her parents' driveway.

"How did you know where they live if I haven't told you?" she asked.

"It's kind of my job to find things like that."

She put a finger to her temple. "Prove it: what am I thinking right now?"

He squinted as he studied her. "I'm going to say it's another joke about my muscles."

She gasped and applauded. "Well done. Amazing."

He glanced at the house, a nondescript little bungalow. "Is there anything I should know about your family?"

She glanced at the house, too, smile slipping. "They're highly conventional; you'll fit in perfectly."

CHAPTER 3

The house was, indeed, conventional, with three bedrooms, two bathrooms, and beige-inspired décor. Josie, who he now realized wore a fuchsia sweater with white flamingoes knitted into it, atop a matching pink skirt, stood out like a speck of neon in the night sky. It didn't take Tristan long to realize it was a metaphor for their entire dynamic as a family. "Exasperated" would be the best word to describe her family's reaction to Josie. Tristan didn't get it. She was a little exuberant and possibly eccentric, but she wasn't shooting heroin into her eyeballs or tattooing rap lyrics on her neck. Compared to the things he'd seen, Josie seemed angelic.

"This is Tristan," she introduced, waving in his direction.

He tensed, bracing himself for the coded looks that always seemed to be exchanged when he met a woman's family, but the Davis family merely gave him tightly controlled polite smiles. He was a little stymied by that, but maybe it was because he had never tried to be friends with a woman before. When he met a girl's parents, it was always because they were dating and it was a logical progression. Maybe this was how the other half lived, the half that could be platonic with the opposite sex.

"Hi," he said and Josie's head whipped in his direction. "What?" he added to her.

"You have teeth," she noted.

"What?"

"Your teeth. I haven't yet seen them. You've never smiled at me, and you dole words like you're being taxed on them each time you take them from your word retirement account. And now you're beaming creepily, and your previously arctic tone is warm and endearing."

"I'm a social chameleon," he told her, reverting to his normally flat tone.

"Or there's some kind of glitch in your programming and I should probably notify the factory that made you," she said.

He touched a finger to her nose and said, "Boop," biting back a smile when she burst into a fit of giggles that shook her shoulders, making the flamingos dance. He wasn't so distracted that he failed to notice her family's reaction to her laughter, notably her older sister who winced and cringed away.

"Josie, settle down," she said, and it was like someone threw a cup of water on Josie, dousing her amusement. Cheeks tinged pink, she cleared her throat and crossed her arms over herself, facing forward.

"Thanks, Janine. I can always count on you to dampen any joy in your radius," Josie said.

"It's called being an adult," Janine said.

"Strange that you've been doing it since birth then," Josie remarked.

"Josie," her mother said.

"What? She started it," Josie said, pointing to her sister.

Her mother gave her a look and Josie pressed her lips together, stuffing down a further reply. "Why don't you take these utensils outside to your father?" She handed Josie a massive tray loaded with grilling implements. Josie took the tray and did a double take at Tristan when he took it from her, relieving her of the burden.

In lieu of commentary, she gave his bicep a little squeeze. He shook his head at her, and she smiled as she reached for the door. Two men stood beside the grill, Josie's father and brother, Bart.

"This is Tristan," Josie introduced with another flourish.

He gave the men a little nod as he set the tray on the table beside the grill.

"You hoodwinked a guy into being your date for a family barbecue?" Bart asked before tossing a piece of watermelon into his mouth.

"This week a family barbecue, next week his power of attorney," Josie said, also reaching for a piece of watermelon. "He's only a pal, though."

"Ah, I thought he looked a little too normal for your usual tastes," Bart said.

"Shows what you know; he's a Brony," Josie said.

"Not a Brony," Tristan contradicted. He grabbed a hank of her hair and gave it a warning tug.

"Sorry," Josie said, smoothing her hair. "He's more of a Cinderella type guy." She jumped out of the way of his hand when it reached for her again.

Her father watched them with an ambivalent sort of smile. "You sure you don't want this one, Josie? I like the look of him better than the last guy."

"The illusionist?" Bart said with a snort.

"That was his hobby, not his job," Josie inserted.

"Doesn't make it better," Tristan said.

Josie rounded on him and made a closing motion with her hand. "You're too new to have an opinion on my love life. And you two stop. We had three dates. I wasn't ready to change my monogram."

"I'm surprised you haven't dated a monogrammer by now," Bart said. "I think it's about the only aimless drifter type you haven't tapped into."

Josie gave an annoyed little cluck. "Sometimes you have to kiss a lot of frogs before you find your prince."

"That one guy actually looked like a frog," Bart said. "He should have his thyroid checked, see if they can do something about those bulgy eyes."

Josie whirled, blocking him from her view. "Dad, are you going to do something about him?"

"He's not saying anything that's not true, Josie. You do tend to date a lot of weirdos." He eyed Tristan, probably trying to discern in which way he might secretly be a weirdo.

"Josie might date some...different sort of guys," Tristan said, picking up the thread of the conversation when he saw an opening, "but it's not like there's been anyone scary, right? No one threatening or creepy, no one you thought might actually hurt or take advantage of her."

Bart and his father eyed each other, thinking. "There was that guy right after high school," Bart said slowly, eyes darting warily to Josie.

Josie pressed her lips together and looked away. It was clear she didn't want to talk about it. On the other hand, she hopefully realized Tristan needed as much information as possible.

"What was wrong with him?"

"She didn't tell you about him?" Bart asked, brows aloft.

Tristan eyed Josie. She bit her lip, eyes suspiciously moist. "She doesn't like to talk about it," he said.

"With good reason," her father said angrily. "That guy almost got her killed."

"Dad," Josie said, shaking her head as she dashed at her eyes.

"Well he did, Josie. That guy was bad news. Goodbye to bad rubbish, I say."

"She broke up with him?" Tristan asked, but the question was met with sudden silence. Finally Josie took a shaky breath and answered.

"No. He died."

The ensuing silence was tense and awkward. Josie sniffed. Tristan caught the sleeve of her sweater and gave it a little tug. "I see a glider over there. Come sit with me," he said, tone soft and gentle.

Josie regarded him with big eyes, then followed him to the glider and sat down. "Thanks for the rescue," she breathed, sounding relieved.

"It wasn't a rescue," he said, tone back to normal. "It was part of my job. I need to know more about the dead boyfriend."

"Why? It was a car accident."

"A guy threatens you and within the year someone close to you dies." He shook his head. "I don't like coincidences like that."

Her lashes fluttered furiously. "You think...you think he was killed? Because of me?"

"I don't think anything yet, that's why I need more information. Tell me everything."

"There's not much to tell. His name was Tony Alexander. He was my bad boy phase."

"*You* had a bad boy phase," he said, reaching out to touch one of the flamingoes on her sweater.

She yanked her sweater back. "Yes, I had a bad boy phase. It was pretty soon after the guy made the threat. I was trying to let go of my fear. I thought if I dated someone scary and dangerous, it might work to eradicate all my fears. Instead it was messy and depressing."

"How messy? How depressing? Were you serious? Did you love him?"

"This is feeling very high school confessional," she said.

"It helps if I can see the big picture. No detail is too small or unimportant. The tiniest thing might crack a case, and you never know what it will be." He pulled out his notebook and pen, poised to write.

"At the time I thought maybe we were serious, I wanted us to be. Later I realized it was a little more than rebelling against my fear; it was rebelling against my family."

"Expound."

"I'm the rogue. They're all prescriptive."

"I wouldn't exactly call you a rebel," he said, touching her sweater again.

"Stop touching my flamingoes," she said and then, realizing how that sounded, flushed crimson and reached to her other side to pick a flower, sniffing it to give herself a pause.

Tristan waited her out.

She lowered the flower and spoke. "Maybe I'm not a rebel in the classic sense, but comparatively I am. My sister and brother always do everything right and perfect. I might get there eventually, but I take a more meandering path; I ask the hard questions no one wants to answer. I resent being told what to do by someone who doesn't have a good reason to back it up, whereas they are yes-men to all authority. So, yes, in my small way, I am very rebellious."

He gave her a little nod, accepting the explanation. "Back to the guy. Don't compare him to you and tell me he was bad; compare him to a crazed serial killer and tell me how he rates."

"He wasn't on hard drugs, that I know of. He probably might have gone that route, if he'd lived longer, because his rebellion was much more blatant than mine. I questioned the envelope and pushed it a little. He tore it to shreds and lit it on fire. He smoked, both cigarettes and occasionally pot. He drank, often to excess and got drunk. At the time I was stupid enough to think those rebellious behaviors made him cool. With perspective I've realized they made him dangerous. I think I was already starting to realize. We'd been having increasingly major disagreements."

"About what?" he asked.

"About how far I was willing to go. We'd barely been dating when he started to pressure me. I wanted him to be my fun fling, not a possible baby daddy. I didn't want to be with him that way. He took it personally."

He gripped the pen, so hard it might have snapped if he didn't consciously release his grasp. "Did he hurt you?"

"No, but he scared me, and he might have eventually. He yelled and threatened a lot. All in all it was a bad experience. Do not recommend the baddie. But at least it cured me of my desire to try again. Give me a silly goober, as long as he's nice, I'll take him."

He didn't say so, of course, but he thought it was unfair of her father and brother to make fun of her so-called goober selections while also disapproving of the one bad boy. One would think they'd be thrilled to have a goofy geek, after the almost disaster.

"Tell me about the accident," he commanded.

"We were at a party. We got in a huge fight, and he left. I called Bart to come get me. The next morning I got the call about Tony's accident, apparently the police interviewed everyone at the party."

"Why?"

"Because he was seriously drunk and we were all underage. I hadn't been drinking, thankfully, so I was off the hook. But it was a good lesson for me, in all the ways." She shuddered.

He took notes. Her gaze shifted to him, watching him intently. "You know, copious note taking shifts you into my lane."

"Which lane is that?" he asked without looking at her.

"Hot nerd."

He coughed.

"Lozenge?" she asked, rooting around in her purse for the little metal tin of them she kept on standby.

He surprised them both by opening his mouth and allowing her to place a lozenge on his tongue.

"If this keeps up, I'm going to have to widen the lanes, maybe put in a bypass," she said and he coughed so hard he sent the lozenge flying across the hedge.

CHAPTER 4

"Is your sister always like that?" Tristan asked as he drove Josie home. It seemed as though her sister had a derisive comment ready to launch each time Josie opened her mouth, more like an enemy combatant than an adult sibling.

"Yes. She's always been like that, probably a big sister/little sister thing. I annoy her bigly. But currently her bad mood has a name called 'pending divorce.' I'm trying to give her space and be patient."

"And your brother, is he always so…"

"Condescending of my life choices? Yep. It's barrels of fun. Hey, you're a good actor. I think everyone totally bought that you were asking questions because you care about me and my life. *I* almost got the warm fuzzies, had to keep reminding myself that you're the job, only ever the job." She made her voice go low like his when she said the last part.

"I never once said that."

"You were thinking it."

They reached her house. She glanced at him in surprise when he parked and took off his seatbelt. "Uh, I'm your security detail," he reminded her.

"Huh. I guess I thought of it more as being for investigatory purposes, rather than protective. Kinda nice, not going to lie. You know what really threatens my wellbeing? My trash. Maybe you could take it out."

He didn't answer.

"I'm only going to ask you this once: Were you or were you not the inspiration behind the song 'Silence is Golden'?"

He continued to ignore her, snatching her keys and using them to unlock her door. When the door was unlocked, she put her hand on the handle, but he put out an arm, blocking her and holding her back. "Why isn't your porch light on?"

"Because I didn't leave it on?"

"It should be on a timer, along with several other outside lights. And you need to do some landscaping. The hedges are a security nightmare." She put her hand on the handle again. Again he pulled her back, this time with a sigh. "I go first."

"I thought ladies were supposed to go first," she muttered, but she stepped back, allowing him to enter the house first and fumble for the light in the total darkness.

"Josie," Tristan said, standing perfectly still.

"Yes, Tristan," Josie replied, a step behind him.

"Memorize what I am about to tell you because it's important: light good; dark bad. Get some timers for indoors and leave some lights on." He finally found the light and flicked it on.

"I'm going to have to sell plasma for my electric bill."

"You're a teacher, I assumed you had to do that already," he remarked, pushing back a smile when she did the little laugh that made her shoulders shake. Her head made a few passes back and forth, taking everything in. He tensed. "What is it? Something different, something wrong?"

"No, I'm merely trying to see it through your eyes. Is it like a robotic scan when you're on the job? Shades of black and white and scary red when you receive an alert?"

He scanned the space, not black and white by any means, but rather a riot of cheerful colors that made him feel unexpectedly cozy. They weren't colors he would ever have put together—hunter green, gold, turquoise, and rose with little pops of red. But somehow they worked and worked well. On the back of the couch was a multi-hewed granny square afghan that made him want to sit down and wrap himself in it. Of course he couldn't and wouldn't, because he was on the job. But maybe when this was over Josie could give him some pointers on decorating. So far since moving to the city his style could best be described as "serial killer on a budget."

"Mind if I sit?" he asked.

"Of course not."

He sat and pulled out his notebook. "I wanted to look through this while everything was fresh, to make certain I didn't miss anything." He began skimming his notes.

Josie plucked off her shoes and sank onto the cushion beside him with a sigh.

"You've had the same friends since high school," Tristan said, apropos of nothing.

"Yes," Josie drawled. "I know you're pretending not to judge me, but I still felt a little condemnation in that question."

"You don't think it's unusual to keep the same friend group from childhood?"

"I'd say it usually falls off because people move around. I never moved, neither did they. Hence we're all still here and still friends. I have other friends, people from work. But the core group is the same." She tipped her head, studying him. "You're not friends with anyone from high school?"

He thought of the kamikaze trail he'd left behind him when he moved and didn't answer. "I'm going to need to meet them," he said instead.

"That's easy enough," she said, resting her head on the back of the couch as she regarded him.

"Stop that."

"Stop what?" she asked.

"You're looking at me like I'm one of your problem kindergarten-ers," he said.

"The people who are hardest to love need it the most," she said.

He shook his head. "Don't try to fix me; I'm not fixable."

Now it was her turn to stare it him in what was becoming disconcerting silence.

He set down his pen, concentration broken. "What do you do for your difficult students?"

"A hug and a lozenge, for starters," she said.

"The lozenge didn't work," he told her.

"Would you like me to try a hug?"

When he didn't respond, she eased closer, stretched out her arms, and paused. "You're not going to rip my arms off, are you?"

"Roll the dice and find out," he said.

She continued forward, slid her arms around him, and gave him a gentle hug. With nowhere for her head to go, it rested on his solid chest, her ear over his heart. He drew in a deep breath.

"Tristan."

"Hmm."

"Are you sniffing me?"

He let out the breath. "Not anymore."

She laughed and sat back, tipping her head to assess him. Maybe it was her imagination, but his shoulders seemed less tense. Maybe the hug had worked a little to soften him or ease his pain. "Do you want a cup of tea?"

Did he? He knew without looking that her kitchen would be overtly cheerful and probably yellow. She would brew tea in a pot and serve it with cookies she would likely call "biscuits." He *would* feel cheered and comforted, probably immensely. He took another breath, said, "No," then stood and let himself out.

CHAPTER 5

The next day Tristan checked the posts he'd put on social media, but they netted nothing more than a few casual comments and the obligatory crackpot or spammer. After that he headed to the police station, intent on looking into two reports: Josie's initial report on the threat and the death of Tony Alexander. It was a pipe dream that they would have kept Josie's statement, especially when nothing came of it, and they hadn't. Five minutes after arriving at the records department, he learned non-felony reports in this jurisdiction were only kept for five years, except in the case of death, in which case they became permanent.

He put in his request, went for lunch, and still had to wait when he came back. Eventually a harried clerk gave him the copy of Tony Alexander's accident report. Too curious to wait, Tristan sat at a chair in the antiseptic lobby and dug in, but there wasn't much substance. It was a one vehicle accident. The kid slid off the road and flipped the car, no skid marks, no witnesses. Post mortem, his blood tested twice the legal limit. The officer had included some party interviews who all agreed the kid was wasted. Josie was noted, but not by name, in a brief statement. "He got crazy mad at his girlfriend, yelling and screaming. He wanted her to go with him, but she said he was too drunk to drive.

We thought he was going to hit her. She cried until someone came to pick her up."

Tristan felt the pucker between his brows and worked to subdue it. The incident happened a decade ago, and the kid was dead. But he didn't like the thought of Josie being in such a vulnerable position, yelled at by a drunk kid, almost in a fatal wreck. Even more than that, he didn't like that he didn't like it. *I am the job, only ever the job,* he reminded himself, but that only worked to make him remember Josie.

He texted her but didn't hear back. Having seen the chaos of her classroom, that wasn't unusual. But he couldn't stop the disconcerted feeling in his gut, the one that would only be reassured by contact. Checking his watch, he decided to make a pass by her school, which would soon be out for the day.

The school's security seemed tight. Not that Tristan thought Josie was in a high level of danger, more than any other teacher, but he was always glad when proper measures were taken. The school was locked. After being let in, he had to show his ID and sign in at the desk, then walk through a metal detector. Class was still in session, and Tristan was strangely happy about that. He told himself it was because it helped him get a big picture view of Josie and her life, but really it was because he wanted to see her interact with the kids, instinctively knowing how it would go.

The door was open, the sound of singing filtering into the hallway. He paused in the door, leaning against the jamb. Josie caught sight of him and gave him a smile, a fleeting one because she had her hands full, literally and with a ukulele. She played a song about the letter E, and the kids sang along. One of them reached over and grabbed his neighbor's arm, giving it a few hard tugs. The kid being tugged tried to ignore him, but it was clear he would soon lose his temper with his neighbor.

"Should we shake out our wiggles?" Josie suggested loudly, momentarily snagging the arm tugger's attention.

"YES," the kids chorused loudly together.

"Everybody up," Josie said. She stood, set the ukulele aside, and put her hands in the air. Giggling, the kids mostly followed suit. The kid tugging the arm and the kid having his arm tugged were once again poking at each other, now ignoring Josie.

"We can't shake out our wiggles until everyone is standing with their hands in the air," she said pointedly, now staring at them. The kids around them became aware they were the cause of the problem and began urging them up. Slowly they stood and put their hands in the air, and Josie's eyes fell on Tristan. "Everyone."

He shook his head.

She remained staring at him with the teacher gaze that made him squirm. He squirmed harder when twenty five year olds whipped their heads to see who she was staring at, now also focusing on him, some of them with wide eyes at his unsmiling too-big appearance. When it became clear she wouldn't back down, and would also soon lose her audience, he put his hands in the air, biting back a smile when the kids started to giggle.

Josie sang a predictably ridiculous song about shaking her sillies out, wriggling her appropriate body parts as the song progressed. The kids followed suit, singing and wriggling and laughing. Occasionally they turned to make certain Tristan was also shaking his sillies, and he dutifully complied, shaking harder when they watched.

The bell rang and Josie clapped her hands together. "Okay, friends. Remember to gather your bags and line up at the door. Line leader, raise your hand."

A little girl jutted her hand into the air, scrambling to grab her bag so she could be the first to stand by the door. She did so, and then remembered Tristan with sudden unease.

"Hi," he said, feeling the massive height disparity between them.

"Hi," she said shyly.

"What's your name?" he asked.

"Leanna. Who are you?"

"I need to see Miss Davis about something."

"Are you going to arrest her?"

"No, of course not. Why would you think that?"

"Aren't you a policeman?"

The question hit unexpectedly hard. Tristan swallowed and shook his head. "No, I'm not."

Josie called their attention again, snagging the girl's focus on her. Tristan eased inside the room so the kids could get out. He stood at the window and watched the organized chaos of dismissal. Eventually Josie came to stand beside him.

"Do they all look like tiny ants to you?" she asked.

Oddly, he had just been thinking that. Not because of their size, but because they all seemed busy and intent. Though it seemed like pandemonium to him, everyone knew where they were going and what they were doing.

He tore his gaze from the window and stared down at her. Today she wore a red dress with a pink cardigan with hearts on the pockets. "You look like a tiny ant to me."

She tipped her head, offering him a smile that was either saucy or ornery, he couldn't decide. "What do you think you look like to me?"

"Are you flirting with me? Is this how a kindergarten teacher flirts?"

"No, that usually involves some sort of craft glue and glitter." Hands on hips, she turned to survey her disaster of a classroom. "You probably know the answer to this: is it a felony to skip town and change my name to avoid cleaning this?"

"Not if you continue to pay your taxes." He unbuttoned his sleeves and rolled them a couple of times. "Tell me where to begin, I'll help."

She sucked in a breath, watching him. "I really did buy the deluxe package."

"We leave no stone unturned and clean up after five year olds," he said.

"Is that a mission statement or a motto?"

"It's a jingle, I'm looking for someone to write the music part. With a ukulele, perhaps?"

She laughed. "Don't look at me. I only know three chords. Turns out it's really hard to keep a group of kindergarteners on track without some sort of instrument, like herding cats. Since I taught myself to play, the attention span during song time has gone up a hundred and twenty percent."

"Yes, but how are their math scores?" he asked.

"They've gone down by the same amount. Pure coincidence, I assure you." she headed toward the crayons again.

"What is it with you and those crayons?" he asked.

"It bothers me when they're disorganized."

He motioned to the complete chaos of the rest of the room.

"Don't try to figure this out." She tapped her forehead. "The depths are too deep. All I know is that I can organize the crayons in ten minutes and make them perfect. Everything else is too far gone."

He began to see what she meant as he attempted to clean up. Sorting things and putting like with like was easier said than done. In the end he moved on to the bigger things, rehanging the curtain that had been torn down, putting chairs back at desks, picking up the blocks and putting them in the bucket.

"Was there a purpose to this visit?" Josie asked. She finished with the crayons and started to wipe down the desks. "Not that you need one, but you seem like a purposeful person."

"I read the death report today on your ex."

She froze. "Did you learn anything?"

"No. I thought it might be worthwhile to talk to the officer who took your initial report after you received the threat." Now he paused and regarded her. "You did do a report, right?"

"I did. Back then I told anyone who would listen, and some who wouldn't, about what happened. The officer appeared to listen. I assume he wrote something up. He told me to keep a watchful eye and report anything suspicious and that was that. I never heard from him again." She gave a helpless shrug.

"What was his name?" Tristan asked, reaching for his notebook.

"I don't know his first name, but his last name was Huggins. Officer Huggins."

Tristan paused and regarded her again. "Huggins?"

"Yes. Don't tell me you know him."

"No, but he's the same officer who did the report for Tony Alexander's accident."

"Is that unusual?" she asked.

"I think so." He tucked his notebook back in his pocket. "I guess he and I will be having a conversation, sooner, rather than later."

"Was that it?" she asked.

"That was it," he affirmed.

"You could have texted."

"I did."

She pulled out her phone and checked the time of the text. "Ah, that was during recess. It's like *Lord of the Flies* then. Sorry. I could have saved you a trip."

"I didn't mind," he said in his flat, deadpan way. "Unless it's a problem for you that I'm here."

"I don't mind," she said, mimicking his tone and expression with scary accuracy. It was rather annoying, he realized, to not be able to read anything in a person's face or voice. They seemed to be having some sort of contest to see which of them would break first. Before they could find a winner, someone spoke from the doorway.

"Yo-yo, Jo-Jo, we still on for Saturday?" A man leaned around the edge of the doorframe so only his head was visible.

"Hey, that cool person slang app you downloaded is paying off in spades," Josie said.

"I know, right? Saturday?"

"Yes," Josie replied with a nod.

"Hey, you look cute. I thought that was your Valentine's outfit. Why are you wearing it so early?"

"I bought a new Valentine outfit. I don't want to give anything away, but purple is involved. It's going to be epic," Josie said.

Tristan shifted, and the guy's attention fastened on him.

"Uh, is this a dad?" the guy asked, eyeing Tristan warily, trying to arrange his features into a more professional demeanor.

"Well, it's not *my* dad," Josie said, laughing when the guy tossed her an annoyed frown. "No, it's not a dad. This is Tristan. Tristan, this is Gabe." She motioned between the men.

"Hey, how do you do," Gabe said. His tone was friendly, but his eyes held a lot of questions.

Tristan gave him an upward nod and straightened, perceptibly more tense.

"Okay," Gabe drawled, head swiveling back to Josie. "So, see you Saturday, Jose."

"See you," she said, tossing him a belated wave he didn't see.

"You dating that guy?" Tristan asked. It was hard to keep the tension out of his voice, but he didn't like wrenches being thrown in his investigation. A boyfriend was definitely a wrench.

Josie chuckled. "No, that's my principal."

"That guy is your boss?" Tristan said, brows aloft.

Josie blinked at him. "Wow, that's the most emotion I've ever seen from you. Apparently the key to cracking you is surprise."

"He didn't seem very bosslike," Tristan added, smoothing his expression again.

"That's because I've known him for eons. Middle school, to be exact. We got the job here together, as teachers. He's only been the principal a couple of years."

"What's on Saturday, if not a date?" Tristan said.

"I ask myself that same question every weekend." She reached for a stack of papers and began sorting. "Gabe and I run with another friend."

"You run?"

She scowled at him. "My self esteem compels me to skip over your blatant shock and answer yes, I run. Not everyday, but it's something I like to do with friends. Those friends specifically."

He studied the door again, thinking. "If you've known them that long, I should probably be there for that."

"If you think you can keep up," she said and giggled with the shoulder shakes at his expression. "Joking. Obviously you're super fit and will have to dumb it down for us mere mortals. Better?"

"You think you're so funny," he said.

"If I don't, who will?" she returned.

"Who, indeed?"

"I enjoy a man who can pull off 'indeed' in the middle of a sentence," she said.

He blinked at her, gaze intent.

"Do you want to grab something to eat?" she offered.

His stomach rumbled with hunger. They could talk more about her case, about her impressions along with his. It didn't have to mean anything more than a working supper. "No," he said and left without saying goodbye.

CHAPTER 6

Josie watched Tristan leave with an odd mixture of disappointment and relief. When she first entered Gaines Hillcrest's office, she knew she'd made the right decision. She had pondered a while, going back and forth on whether it was a good use of her grandfather's inheritance money. But after one too many nights of broken sleep, she realized she couldn't remember what it felt like to not wake up in a cold sweat, heart pounding, assimilating the house sounds to make certain no one was there, that the scary bad man hadn't found her at last. Gaines had welcomed her with a warm smile, allaying her worries with a comforting tilt of his head. *Don't discount your gut,* he'd said, pointing to a sweet picture on his desk, his wife and kids. *My wife had a stalker. The police didn't believe her, but it turned out to be true.*

She had breathed a little easier that day, up until the moment he told her he'd be handing off her case to someone else. *Unfortunately I'm already attached to another job, but you'll like this guy. He's a honey badger, relentless. I wouldn't give him your case if I didn't trust him completely.*

It was possible he'd merely been blowing smoke, but he was so warm and comforting she chose to believe he had her best interest at heart. And then she met Tristan.

Her first impression wasn't great, if she were being honest. Tall, well built, and stoic might be bonuses in the world of private security, but they had never appealed to Josie. She liked people who were approachable and soft, maybe even a little self-deprecating. *People like me.* Tristan had been so cold and aloof. She thought surely they wouldn't be a good match to work together on her case. Either he would think she was a crackpot or a liar. But she had to give him his due; not only had he been professional and objective, he was turning out to be more complex than she first thought.

Sometimes when he looked at her, it was like he was hungry. Maybe even starving, and she held the last crust of bread. But when she tried to edge closer and advance their friendship, he flatly rejected her. He was a puzzle and, she could readily admit, ridiculously attractive. Not that she cared much about that. Eye candy was usually better to look at than consume. And she had learned her lesson about bad boys the hard way with no need to ever repeat it. Was Tristan bad, though? Or merely distrusting and standoffish? Was that any better than volatile and insecure?

She wasn't attracted to him. Was she? She hadn't been, not at first glance. What she told him was true—he wasn't her type. She liked nice guys who were a little goofy, a little awkward. But last night when Tristan tugged her toward the glider, it was almost like he was defending her from her family, providing her an emotional reprieve. *He said he wasn't,* she reminded herself. *He said it was only about the job.* And then he'd pulled out the little notebook and started to write, and what she said was true: she could see his intelligence in that moment, and it was more attractive than anything that came before. Smart men were her bread and butter, and Tristan was undoubtedly smart, not a meathead like she'd first thought.

Not that any of it mattered. She was clearly not *his* type, a fact he hadn't contradicted when she said it the first time they met. And his obvious disbelief in her ability to run drove the point home further. He was doubtless looking for a fellow gym bunny, something that could never describe Josie. She liked to work out, but she wasn't relentless about it. It was one of those things she did when she remembered or needed to burn some stress or excess calories. She certainly wasn't stringent or religious about it, not like Tristan, whose devotion to the gym was obvious by the perfection of his physique.

At first those perfect muscles had been a turnoff for Josie. In her experience men who put that much energy and effort into their bodies had little energy or effort for anything else. Tristan, though…

She stared at the door, not seeing it, trying to puzzle the man who'd just left, not realizing at first that another man was now standing there until he spoke.

"Who was the guy?"

She jumped and put a hand to her heart, blinking Gabe into focus. "What?"

He thumbed toward the door. "The guy. Who?"

"He's someone I know. He stopped by to ask me a question."

"Does he not have a phone?"

"He does, but you know how it goes. I was a little out of touch." She held her phone aloft with a little shake.

"Sounds needy," Gabe said.

Josie sighed, weary of the cycle they'd been in since middle school. Anytime Josie was single, Gabe ignored her, treating her like the pal she was. Anytime another guy showed interest, he puffed up and started acting jealous, an act that would continue exactly until the guy was gone. "You'll have plenty of time to get to know him better. He's coming with us on Saturday for our run."

"As what, the drill instructor? That guy is huge."

"Yes, yes he is."

"Is that what you're into now?" Gabe asked, tone resentful. "Guys who look like The Rock?"

"Yes, Gabe. I've discarded twenty eight years of depth in favor of hotness."

"Don't lower your standards because you've been in a dry spell and you're feeling desperate," Gabe said.

"Great life advice for both of us. Tell me about that last girl you dated, the one who sold pictures of her feet to strangers," Josie said.

"She was providing a much-needed service for lonely old men," he said, pointing a finger at her. "All I'm saying is that you should be careful. You tend to fall full throttle for losers. Remember Tony?"

"More and more lately. Were you at the party that night? I can't remember."

He looked away, squinting as he stared out the window. "Everyone was at the party that night. It was the place to be."

"What do you remember?"

He tore his gaze off the window and directed it on her. "I remember you crying, a lot. I remember being relieved that you weren't in that car with him when he died. I remember..."

"What?" she prompted when he stopped.

He took a breath and continued. "I remember feeling bad for how relieved I was that he was gone. I know that's bad, but I'm not the only one who felt that way."

She knew that to be true because she'd felt it herself, a combination of profound sadness and relief. She didn't want Tony to be dead, but she also felt like she'd found an escape hatch for something that was beyond her control. Even before that disastrous night things had felt like they were spiraling to doom, but she'd been powerless to stop them. Tony hadn't wanted to let her go, a fact he'd told her on numerous occasions. *You're the only one who gets me, the only one who loves me, Josie. I can't ever lose you.* She had never told him she loved him, had never come close to promising him forever. Josie's stomach churned, remembering the strange mix of fear and elation she'd felt then. She had known at the time his behavior was unhealthy, but there had been a not-so-little part of her—the teenage girl part—that had enjoyed the high drama of everything.

For once Josie had been the center of attention and gossip, had felt the intense ups and downs of first romance. And then Tony died and everything was flat and gray again. It was years before she felt ready to date again, and everything since had been...bland, easy, simple. *Maybe that's why it never seems to last; maybe you need more than bland, easy, and simple.* Tristan flashed through her mind and she shook her head to dislodge the image. He would not be bland, easy, or simple. But he would also be the epitome of unrequited love. While it might be true that Josie needed a little bit more adventure than she currently had in her life, she did not need heartbreak and desperation, two things that hovered over Tristan with an almost discernable aura.

"What made you ask if I remembered Tony's death?" Gabe asked, alerting her to the fact that he was still there.

She blew out a breath, trying to clear her mental cobwebs. "I guess I've been thinking about the past a lot lately, trying to put to bed some old ghosts."

"Huh," Gabe said. Josie resumed tidying her room, not realizing that Gabe watched her long after she was aware.

CHAPTER 7

Tristan dressed with care, on the night he was set to meet with Josie's friends from high school. They were all women, and he wasn't averse to using his assets to make a good impression. He wondered if he would finally get to see Josie in something other than some version of a skirt or dress, but that was exactly what she wore when she answered the door, a black pencil skirt with a pale blue sweater. The only difference with this one was that the sweater was belted at the waist, conforming nicely to her hourglass figure.

"Is this spray painted on?" Josie whispered, trailing a finger over the sleeve of his t-shirt.

"Is this?" he asked. He hooked a finger on the belt of her sweater, giving it a tug that sent her stumbling a step closer, erasing the small distance between them. They stared at each other, aware their fingers were still on the other's body but unaware how to disengage. "I think your poker face is improving." Beyond her eyes, her expression gave nothing away.

"Maybe yours is getting worse," she said. He wasn't smiling, but did his face look less frosty and stoic than usual, or was that her overheated imagination?

"Nope," he said, his thumb joining his index finger to caress her waist.

"Hmm," she replied while her other fingers curved around his impressive bicep. "Must be in my head."

"Nothing gets in the way, when I'm on the job," he said. His thumb was doing something magic by her navel. She tipped forward, gripping his bicep now for support.

"You're a consummate professional," she said softly, now staring at his lips. *Pretty lips,* she thought, which was absurd considering there was nothing pretty about him. He was too masculine for that. But still she stared at them, marveling at their sculpted perfection.

"Jo-Jo, where'd you go? Did you get abducted?" someone called from the other room, startling them apart.

Josie snapped to attention and yanked back her hand, facing the living room. "Be right there." To Tristan she added, "Ready?"

He gave her a little upward nod. She realized his expression looked exactly the same as it had a minute ago, exactly the same as it had since she met him—a flat affect that gave nothing away. Had she misconstrued their earlier moment somehow? Had she gripped his bicep because she thought she sensed something that wasn't there? Her face flushed with mortification, certain that must be it. How awkward, especially because she wasn't even sure she liked him, outside of his overt attractiveness. How could she? She knew nothing about him beyond his name and the fact that he filled out a t-shirt like it had been custom designed for him. Liking someone based solely off appearances was so foreign to her it made her feel icky for its shallowness. She vowed to keep an extra layer of emotional distance between them for the remainder of the evening, striving for a breezy tone when she introduced him to her friends.

"Guys, this is Tristan." Josie paused inside the room, Tristan beside her. Her group of friends had known each other forever and were lively, often talking over each other to be heard. But as soon as Tristan entered the chat there was dead silence. All eyes fastened on him, and a couple of jaws dropped.

"Josie, did…did you hire a stripper?" Natalie asked.

Josie gasped and pressed her hand over her eyes. "Natalie. No, absolutely no. Tristan is…he stopped by to…" She dropped her hand and trailed off, tossing him a helpless look.

"I needed to drop something off," he said, holding a bag aloft, one Josie had previously failed to notice.

"What?" she blurted, too flustered to remember she was probably supposed to already know.

In lieu of an answer, he handed her the bag. She poked her head in and laughed out loud. "Lozenges." There were probably a dozen boxes in the bag.

"A variety of flavors, recipe research," he said.

"This is amazing, thank you," she said, beaming at him over the top of the bag. Someone cleared her throat, alerting them to the fact that they had gotten caught up staring at each other.

"Sorry," Tristan said, "I didn't mean to intrude. I can see myself out."

"Uh, no. Let's have you stay," Natalie suggested. "Sit down and catch us up on everything we've missed." Her gaze turned pointedly to Josie who gave a helpless shrug in return. She thought they were going to play Tristan off as a friend, but this felt like more than that.

Everyone shifted, leaving two small spots on the couch for Tristan and Josie, more like a spot and a half. Tristan took up most of the space. Josie accidentally elbowed him as she tried to squeeze in.

"Sorry," she said.

"It's fine," he replied. He gave her leg a pat and left his hand on her knee. She stared at it, along with everyone else in the room.

"So, Tristan," Ellie began. "Tell us how you know our girl, Josie, here. Our silent girl, who apparently keeps everything to herself." Now it was Ellie's turn to toss her a pointed glance, one that promised lots of questions and possibly some retribution later.

"A mutual acquaintance introduced us," Tristan said smoothly.

"Who?" Jenna demanded. They knew everyone Josie knew, after all.

"Gaines Hillcrest. My boss, actually. He thought Josie and I would hit it off," Tristan said. He stretched the truth so smoothly it was like watching someone in a YouTube video make noodles—soothing and a little awe-inspiring.

"And how long have you known each other?" Bridget added.

"Not long," Tristan said. "What about you? How long have you all known Josie?"

"Forever," they chorused together.

Tristan swiveled to inspect Josie. "Yeah? So maybe you can tell me what Josie was like, back in the day. Was she always so…distinct?"

"In one way or another," Natalie said.

"How so?" he asked, turning his attention back to them. If they noted the weird intensity in the question, they didn't let on.

"She didn't develop this style until later in the game," Ellie waved a hand toward Josie. "But she always stood out in some way, liked to be different and set apart."

"Have you met her family?" Jenna asked.

"I did," Tristan said, and their eyes swung accusingly to Josie again. So many unspoken questions in those eyes.

"Then you understand," Bridget said.

"What do you mean?" Tristan asked, tipping his head with either feigned or genuine interest.

"They had certain expectations. Act a certain way, get certain grades. Josie didn't like that mold. She couldn't seem to help but get good grades," Jenna said.

"Because she's stupid smart," Natalie interjected, tossing a piece of popcorn at Josie.

"But she didn't like being pigeonholed into the smart kid role. So she was always searching for another. She tried theater, band, journalism, skiing." Jenna paused and regarded the group. "Am I missing anything?"

"Let's not forget the belly dancing phase," Natalie added.

Tristan swiveled to eye Josie.

"Let's," she said, pointedly ignoring his gaze.

"She's our jack of all trades," Bridget said, smiling fondly at Josie.

"And master of none," Josie said.

"You're pretty good at knitting and crochet," Ellie added loyally.

"My granny skills are on point," Josie agreed.

"A belly dancing granny," Tristan said, and the group laughed as Josie shook her head.

"I don't like where this imagery is headed," Josie said.

"What about guys she's dated? She's been a little cagey there," Tristan said, addressing the group with a conspiratorial tone they lapped up with a spoon. They were all too ready to throw Josie to the wolves if it meant capturing the interest of this hardy hunk of man flesh. Josie had vastly underestimated how much they would enjoy this particular torture session, but she hadn't thought Tristan would play it as her potential love interest; she thought he'd be a new friend, as he had been the night he met her family. Now, as if to further the illusion, he gave Josie's knee a reassuring little pat, inching his hand a tiny bit farther north, toward her thigh. His thumb swept over the inside of her leg, somewhere between tickle and torture.

"Oh, does anyone have the list?" Natalie groaned, turning to survey her friends.

"It is not that long," Josie argued, adding to Tristan, "Honestly, I've pretty much told you everyone pertinent."

"You're probably only counting guys who were official, totally leaving out all the will-we-or-won't-we drama. Josie was into liking boys far before the rest of us."

"You've all caught up admirably," Josie told them, dodging a pillow a heavily pregnant Jenna tossed at her head.

"Fine, let's stick to the notable ones," Bridget said.

"I already told him about Tony," Josie said, and the group shared a collective sneer.

"Did you tell him about Gabe?" Natalie said.

"Gabe your principal?" Tristan asked, turning to survey her again. His expression hadn't changed, but she somehow sensed his annoyance. Probably because he was the meticulous sort who didn't like to leave details to chance.

"Gabe and I have never once gone out," Josie said.

"I'm sorry, did you say gone out or made out?" Ellie said, and everyone *oooohed* in unison.

"I hate you all," Josie told them.

"But not Gabe," Natalie said, snorting when Josie tossed the pillow she was clutching at her.

"That was high school," Josie said.

"And college," Bridget said.

"And when you both got hired," Jenna added helpfully.

"You people know too much," Josie told them, feeling more than a little self-conscious over Tristan knowing this information. He did try to warn her he would dig up her skeletons. Somehow she hadn't quantified her ill-fated attraction to Gabe as a skeleton, and she should have. It was a train wreck and always had been.

"What about the thing?" Tristan said. Josie wondered if he purposely said it that way to assess how big of a deal it was to other people. Judging by the way her friends became immediately still and silent, it was a big deal, indeed.

"That was freaky," Jenna said at last.

"I had nightmares for months," Bridget agreed.

"None of you had any ideas about it? Nothing similar happened to any of you?"

They shook their heads slowly.

"I thought maybe…" Natalie started and broke off.

"You thought what?" Tristan prodded.

Natalie glanced apologetically at Josie and continued. "I thought maybe it was a prank by her brother, for her eighteenth or something."

"Was there a reason you thought that?"

Natalie gave a helpless little shrug. "Lots of us have brothers, and they're a pain. But Bart always seemed to take it to the next level, as if there was vital information he *had* to impart, and it infuriated him when Josie didn't learn what he wanted her to learn, when she took any step out of line. I thought maybe it was an elaborate 18th birthday prank, to teach her a lesson on stranger danger or something. But then when she got so upset, so totally freaked out either he regretted it and wouldn't fess up or he really had nothing to do with it."

"Did anyone ask him?" Tristan asked, addressing Josie this time.

Josie looked a little gobsmacked, staring at Natalie like it was the first time she'd ever heard her brother accused.

"I don't know," Josie said. "I don't know who the police interviewed. I don't know what my dad's response to everything was, besides telling me to let it go. Everything is a little blurry. As Natalie said, I was pretty freaked out."

"How freaked out?" Tristan asked, eyes on her. His thumb kept up its soothing motion on her leg, grounding her. She focused on that, tamping down the old fear, the one that could easily send her into a panic spiral. "Did you pass out? Lose consciousness?"

Josie swallowed hard, blinking tears away. She nodded. "At first I was stunned and disbelieving, a little in shock that it happened, that a person really said those words to me. But after the initial shock wore off, I...I sort of broke down. When I got home and was trying to tell my family what happened, I cried so hard I hyperventilated and, yes, I passed out. Not long enough to be concerning. I didn't go to the hospital. My mom put a cool cloth on my head. Bart got me a paper bag, and I rallied. After that..." She broke off, turning away from everyone's inspection.

"After that what?" Tristan prodded, tone gentle. She could feel her friends staring at her. It was embarrassing to tell them how bad it had been, how bad it still was.

"After that they didn't want me to talk about it or mention it again. They kept urging me to let it go so we could all move on and get over it. Any time I tried to bring it up, they got angry."

"They don't like emotion, and they hate it when Josie shows any not from the pre-approved list," Jenna said, sounding frustrated on Josie's behalf.

"That's what she has us for," Bridget said, tone intentionally light to bring up the mood. "We supply all the emotion and then some."

Josie nodded, dashing at her brimming eyes.

"It was a rough time," Natalie chimed in. "I'm glad it's over."

Josie stared doggedly ahead, and Tristan turned purposefully away. It wasn't over, not by a long shot. But after this, she would let it go. This would be the closure she desperately needed, and she would pay any price, even if it meant she had to hear her friends ask questions about Tristan for the rest of their lives. She put her hand on his, giving it a little pat—of thankfulness. Even if she was paying him, she was glad he was here, glad he was doing this. She was so ready to get on with her life and put this old fear to rest. Beyond ready, really. After this investigation she'd be happy to never talk about it again.

"I should go," Tristan said. "It was great to meet you all, I really enjoyed it." They all bought the statement, regardless of the fact that he didn't smile and there was no warmth in his tone. Josie wondered if people heard what they wanted to hear, her included because her heart fluttered a little when Tristan picked up her hand and brought it to his lips. "Walk me out?"

She nodded, swallowing hard past the renewed embarrassment of having her closest friends witness this false scene. She had brought this on herself, but it didn't make it any less difficult.

Tristan stood and pulled her up beside him, keeping her hand as he led her to the door.

"Was that helpful?" she whispered. "Did you gain anything from that?"

He studied her, thinking, processing. Eventually he gave a little nod.

She smiled. "Not going to tell me?"

"It will be in my report, Miss Davis."

The affect didn't change, but she somehow knew he was teasing her and smiled. "Since you're so much better at subterfuge, do you have any advice for me when I go back in there? They're going to have so many questions; I'll be eaten alive. They're going to wonder why I've been holding out on them and keeping you under wraps."

He eyed her, thinking some more. Eventually he said, "Tell them I'm into you, but you're not into me."

"That's good, and also completely self-sacrificing. How'd you come up with it?" she asked.

"When possible, Josie, it's always best to go with the truth." He brushed his lips on the hand he still held, let it go, and disappeared before Josie could fathom a response.

CHAPTER 8

Tristan made an appointment with Officer Huggins, the man who handled Josie's case a decade ago. Cops fell into different types; old cops were even more distinct. Generally they did not enjoy young upstarts and pretty boys, both things Tristan expected to hear and feel when he met the senior officer. But to his pleasant surprise, Huggins seemed jolly and affable. Finding an officer who'd been serving so many years who remained joyful and optimistic about humanity was about as likely as seeing a two-horned narwhal. Tristan took it for the gift it was, vowing to treat the man with due respect and not take up too much of his time.

"Had to look up the case you were talking about in my private files. You think you won't forget stuff like that, comes as a shock when you do," Huggins said, tapping his temple. He had a big belly and white hair and two years left until retirement. Something told Tristan he would probably spend much of his retirement time playing mall Santas.

"Happens to the best of us," Tristan assured him, helping himself to a seat at the table in the interview room.

"Little Josie Davis. Cute kid, scared out of her mind. Made me feel bad, if I'm being honest. Brought out the dad in me." He sighed, put on a pair of reading glasses, and picked up the report Tristan had brought, playing trombone with the paper, even with the glasses.

"What made you believe her?" Tristan asked.

"Who says I did?" Huggins said and shrugged. "Believe her or not, it had to be investigated."

"*Did* you believe her?" Tristan asked.

Huggins smiled. "I did, actually, but only because I knew too much about the kind of scum that would prey on a young kid like that. You can imagine the pleasure the guy took. Seeing a cute, innocent young girl who looked like Josie, deciding to pull a Michael Myers *Halloween* type scare on her. Sick world. Wish we could have caught him. Even with all the surveillance we didn't catch sight of him." He shrugged as if to say, *What are you going to do?*

"Did you note anything unusual among her family and friends in the course of your investigation, anything your gut told you that you didn't want to commit to paper?"

Huggins let out a breath that smelled strongly of burnt coffee. "Her family was wound real tight. And they seemed reticent, almost...*ashamed* to have me ask questions. Their daughter received such a fright she was on the verge of a nervous breakdown, and they wanted me to go away because it embarrassed them to have their names attached to something like that."

"What about the friends?"

"As far as I could tell, they were squeaky clean. Sometime later there was a boyfriend."

"Who died in an accident," Tristan supplied.

Huggins squinted at him, understanding passing between them. "Odd, right? I asked to do the investigation because of the connection to Josie's case. It was a little too coincidental, you know? Most people go their whole lives without ever talking to the police, yet this kid is involved twice in a year, both times as a bystander or victim. It didn't sit right."

"Did you find anything to tie the two cases together?"

"Anything besides Josie, you mean? No, nothing. She didn't even know Tony Alexander when the guy stopped and threatened her, and his death was an open and shut one car drunk driving accident."

"Your tone and expression tell me you still don't like something there."

"What I don't like is that I never felt closure with either thing. The kid was drunk, the kid had an accident, the end. But..."

"But?"

"The ease of it bothered me, the lack of skid marks bothered me. It was a little *too* open and shut, you know what I mean? If someone wanted to stage the perfect accident, that would be it. Mean, drunk kid, no witnesses, middle of the night, middle of nowhere, cover of darkness. And the Josie thing..." He huffed a sigh. "I could tell it was still bothering her. Every time I saw or talked to her she seemed paler, hands shakier, pupils wider. But her family put so much pressure on her to let it go. It was like I could see her trying to pull herself together for their sake. I wish I could have done more to find the guy, to show her he was an evil crackpot who got a thrill scaring a cute kid."

"That's really all you believe it was?" Tristan said.

Huggins gave a nod. "For a couple of years I held my breath each time we hooked a Jane Doe DOA, scared it would be Josie. But nobody bides their time this long. I hope she's found peace." There was a question in the statement and his brows rose.

Was Josie peaceful? She was settled; she had a house, job, and family. But Tristan sensed a restlessness in her, a discord that had never found complete release. "I'm going to help her find it," he said, a promise to them both.

"If there's anything more I can do..." Huggins let the offer hang.

"I appreciate it," Tristan said sincerely. "I'm going to turn over all the old rocks. It might be handy to have your perspective as the first person who turned them over."

He stood and shook the older man's hand, impressed by the still-strong grip. After giving him his card in case he thought of anything else, he let himself out and sat in his car, staring through the windshield without seeing.

Huggins had believed Josie, that was a relief. At least she hadn't had to go through the pain of being gaslighted by the police, of having her fear diminished by them. Her family, on the other hand… Why had they been so threatened by the investigation? Did they not want Josie to get help? Or, worse, did they not believe her? They thought she was prone to drama and, compared to them, she was. She had tried on several identities in high school before finding one that took, but lots of kids did that. There had been no harm in Josie's many activities, all school-sanctioned projects. The only potential harm had been her selection of a dating partner, and that had ended abruptly and, dare he admit it, tidily. Almost as if someone tied it up in a little bow.

What was it Josie's friends had said about her brother? *Bart seemed to take it personally when Josie stepped out of line…it infuriated him when Josie didn't learn what he wanted her to learn.* Infuriated him enough to take care of the blemish before it could become a bigger stain?

Tristan started the car. It was time to have a little chat with Bart Davis.

⚷

*B*art Davis, CPA, worked in an upscale office in downtown DC. He drove a conservative sedan and dressed in a conservative suit. Even his haircut was tastefully conservative—not long, but not so short it was a buzz. Merely the perfect amount for a man trying to stay in his lane and not stand out.

Tristan watched his office for a while, running some background in his car. The firm in question did reputable work for reputable companies, no shell corporations, nothing funneled to the Caymans, and no secret government work on the side. There was absolutely nothing suspicious in the man's life. He had a serious girlfriend, the same one he'd had for the past year. He lived a quiet life, paid his taxes, and that was all. So why did Tristan get the feeling there was more going on with him?

The workday ended and the lot started to clear. Not surprisingly Bart was in the middle group of workers who left, not the first and not the last. It was as if he intentionally scripted his life to be as mediocre as possible so as not to attract any undue attention. For some reason that set Tristan's teeth on edge, at least in regard to Josie. Was he so married to his mediocrity that he would resent a sister who tried to draw him into the light of unwanted attention? That was a stretch, but there was definitely an odd dynamic there.

Bart drove to the market. Tristan parked a row away and followed him inside, glad for the post-work rush that allowed him to remain unnoticed.

Apparently Bart lacked a supper plan because he meandered a while, vacillating between the salad bar and the frozen section before finally selecting a couple of the healthier frozen meals and putting them in his basket. Tristan stood in the cheese aisle, the one Bart was forced to pass on his way to the checkout. He stared unseeingly at a wheel of gouda, his hand extending as if pondering. Bart passed him, stopped, and backed up.

"Tristan, right?"

Tristan looked at him and gave a little start of surprise. "Oh, hey. Josie's brother. How's it going?"

"Good. Is this your market?"

"Nah, I had a work thing downtown and got hangry. Had a protein slump, you know? What about you? You live downtown?"

"Yes, and my office is right around the corner. This is my go-to for a sad, single man supper." He held his frozen meals aloft.

"Sounds like we're both starved," Tristan said. "Want to grab a burger?"

Bart's smile looked friendly with no wariness or reserve. "Sounds good, a whole lot better than this garbage. Let me put it back, I'll meet you at the front."

Tristan deferred their meal selection to Bart, since it was his turf. They walked to their cars and met a few minutes later at a nondescript little bar Bart assured him had the best burgers. Inside smelled promising, but since Tristan wasn't there for the food, he didn't actually care.

They grabbed a booth at the back and placed their orders. "So how did you and Josie meet? If she said, I don't remember," Bart began after handing the waitress his menu.

"A mutual friend introduced us," Tristan said.

Bart stared at him, waiting for more.

Tristan stared back, unwilling to divulge unless prodded.

"Which friend?" Bart finally said.

"Gaines Hillcrest."

Bart squinted. "I don't know the name."

"Do you know all her friends?" Tristan asked with a little laugh to soften the question.

"Yes," Bart said. "She's always had the same friends. Only her work friends are new, and I've met them. Sometimes she tries to hide her boyfriends. Did she date this guy?"

"Nah, he's happily married," Tristan said.

"Where'd she meet him?"

"You'd have to ask her about that."

Bart studied him through slightly narrowed eyes.

Tristan gave another little laugh, letting some of his discomfort eke through. "I don't think I've ever known this much about my sister."

Bart let out a breath and tried to visibly relax the tense set of his shoulders. He shoved a hand through his hair. "Josie is seven years younger. I guess I sort of took on a parental role, never really shook it."

"Have you guys always been close?" Tristan asked.

"I guess it depends on what you mean by close."

Tristan's brows rose questioningly, hoping to prod him to continue.

"Josie is the baby, you know? And she totally lived up to the role, being as cute and ornery as you can imagine. It was like she had a special talent for trouble. She would always be that kid who tripped and fell into the barbed wire, who stepped on a hornet's nest or landed on a piece of glass."

"Sounds like she kept you busy," Tristan said.

"Yeah, especially because our dad wasn't around much. He traveled a lot for his job."

There was something there, something in his tone. Their food arrived. They spent some time arranging their plates and Tristan circled back around. "Did you feel like the dad, with your dad being away so much?"

Bart nodded. "Two little sisters will do that to you, I guess. Janine's always been straightforward and self-maintaining, but Josie..." He trailed off.

"But Josie," Tristan said, a little fondly, a little leading, but it didn't go anywhere. Bart spent a few minutes biting and chewing his sandwich. Tristan tried another track. "Did your mom work, too?"

"Yeah, I was pretty much their fulltime babysitter." He picked up his straw, stirring absently at his drink.

"Doesn't sound like it was fun to be you," Tristan noted.

"When you're the oldest kid, I don't think you get a say in whether life is fun or not, in how much responsibility you get handed. It is what it is. I never minded until..." he trailed off again, looking even more pensive.

Leading and prodding weren't helping; Tristan decided to be blunt. "Did something happen?"

Bart gave him a frank gaze. "What I'm about to tell you, Josie doesn't know, *can't* know."

"I can't promise to keep things from Josie," Tristan said, not least of which because she was paying him to find things.

"I think when I tell you you'll understand and agree." He took a breath, let it out, and started to talk.

"All the traveling my dad did, it wasn't without consequence." His eyes flicked to Tristan's to see if he got the gist.

"He had an affair?"

Bart nodded. "For a couple of years, apparently."

"Geez," Tristan said, with honest shock this time. This hadn't been in any of the paperwork, probably because Josie didn't know. "How old was Josie?"

"About five. When my mom found out, things got ugly. First they fought. Josie remembers that part, I think. What she doesn't know is that they separated for about eight months. They were both on the fence about whether or not they wanted to make things work. Eventually they did, obviously. Dad broke it off, Mom forgave him with the caveat that he stop traveling. He did. To my knowledge nothing has happened since."

"Why was Josie kept in the dark?"

"She was so little and cute, such a ball of energy and fun. She became our light in the darkness. We all sort of relied on her to keep us going. I credit her with bringing Mom and Dad back together, honestly. She made them laugh when we didn't have much to laugh at. I guess none of us wanted to risk losing or damaging that which made her special, you know? There was a certain...*innocence* about her, untouched by everything bad that happened. Still is, even after everything. Makes me sort of extra protective, I guess." He gave a little shrug and resumed eating.

Tristan took a few bites, deciding where to go next. That definitely explained Bart's odd protective vibe, as well as the weird family dynamic Tristan hadn't been able to put his finger on. "It must have been scary and upsetting when she dated Tony."

Bart huffed an aggrieved sigh. "You have no idea. And the worst part, the absolute worst, was that I *liked* him. I approved of him. I thought he was better than some of the other losers and weirdos she dated. But it turned out that, like most abusers, he was good at putting up a front, at playing his part. He schmoozed and charmed us to the point that..." he trailed away again, but this time Tristan didn't have to prod. He set down his sandwich. "To the point that we sometimes took his side over Josie's. More than once I intervened, told her she was being unreasonable or clingy. Can't tell you how much I regret that now."

"Was it kind of a relief when he died?"

"Not kind of, full on joy. Good riddance to bad rubbish." He took an angry bite of his sandwich.

"If you were fooled by him at first, how did you figure out what was going on? What did he do to reveal himself?"

"Nothing, at least not in my view. One of Josie's friends came to me and told me what was going on."

"Which friend?" Tristan asked.

"Gabe," Bart said, and popped the last bite of his burger.

CHAPTER 9

The weather was starting to turn. There was a slight chill in the air, enough to make the prospect of an early morning run a pleasant one, even on a Saturday. Tristan arrived at the designated meeting place early, both to stretch and for the advantage it would give him to be the first one there. It was a petty power play, but he needed to observe Gabe's reactions on a number of issues.

Yesterday's conversation with Bart had cleared up a few questions, while giving Tristan a few more to answer.

Who, for instance, had Josie's father had an affair with? Had that woman also been married? Might her husband have been angry enough to threaten his wife's lover's child? Had her dad really broken it off when he said he did, never to contact the woman again?

And then there was Gabe, a prominent feature in Josie's life, so prominent that both her friends and family mentioned her attachment to him. Why had he told Bart about Tony? Was it because he knew Bart would do something about it? For that matter, *had* Bart done something about it? Was he responsible for Tony's accident that night? How far would he go to protect his beloved little sister? There had been so much to discuss that somehow Tristan never got around to it. Instead he kept picturing Josie's face and what would happen to her smile if she ever found out the truth about her family. On the other hand, didn't she deserve to know? Was it ethical to keep it from her if she was paying him to find things out? Or should he keep it from her since it wasn't relevant to the investigation? But what if it was relevant to the investigation? Was it ever okay to keep a secret of that magnitude?

In Tristan's experience, secrets were always corrosive, even well-intentioned ones. Look what this secret had already done to the Davis family. Bart had exhausted himself trying to keep it from Josie the last two decades. Her parents had undoubtedly refused Officer Huggins' interference with Josie's threat investigation because they didn't want her to know about her father's affair. What further damage had it done to her, to all of them? On the other hand, it wasn't Tristan's secret to tell. Hearing it from him might make things worse instead of better.

What bothered him most of all was that he cared one way or the other. Josie was only ever supposed to be the job, and now she had become more. Now she had become a real person with real feelings, feelings Tristan might decimate by tossing this Molotov cocktail of revelations into her life.

"I should have known you were the early sort."

Josie spoke from behind him now. He whirled, half expecting to see her in one of her ubiquitous skirts or dresses. Instead she wore regular running gear, stretchy pants and a zip up hoodie, hair in a ponytail.

"You look cute," he blurted.

"Thanks," she said, blushing faintly. She glanced down, as if she'd forgotten what she was wearing and needed the reminder. Or maybe she was trying to see herself through his eyes, to figure out what he saw when he looked at her. He could tell her, but he wouldn't. *The job, only the job.* "You look, um..." She seemingly ran out of words and rested her hand on his bicep, giving it a squeeze. "Won't you get cold in a t-shirt?"

"My thermostat is apparently stuck on overdrive," he told her. "Why? Are you cold?"

"A teensy bit," she said.

He took a step closer, erasing the space between them. "You can borrow some of my warmth."

She stared up at him, eyes wide with…something, he had no idea. She drew in a breath and opened her mouth to respond.

"Josie beat us, alert the media," Gabe declared, coming up beside them. "That must be your doing." He tipped his head toward Tristan who regarded him in stony silence.

"I have never once been late for school," Josie told him, pivoting a step away from Tristan.

Gabe held up his thumb and index finger. "Skin of your teeth sometimes, Davis."

"Who's the big guy?" another man stepped out of his car and joined them. He looked like Bart had described many of Josie's exes—goofy and a little awkward, his teeth a bit too prominent for his mouth, but not freakish or unattractive. Enough to attract a girl who liked interesting guys, a girl like Josie. Was this another ex?

"This is Tristan," Josie said, placing her hand on his bicep again. "Tristan, this is Eli."

"Josie has a new guy?" Eli directed the question to Gabe, said in such a way that he was checking Gabe's okayness with that.

"So it seems," Gabe said.

"You look squinty and suspicious," Josie said, poking Gabe.

"How come you don't say anything to him when he looks squinty and suspicious?" he said, motioning toward Tristan.

Josie tipped her head, inspecting Tristan. "Maybe because I like him squinty and suspicious." She squeezed Tristan's bicep.

"I just threw up in my mouth a little," Gabe said, pressing his hand to his stomach.

"I think that's what Josie said last time you guys made out," Eli said and everyone looked at Tristan when he coughed.

"It's alive," Eli said, noting Tristan's once again flat expression.

"Nothing dead could be so warm," Josie said, easing closer with a shiver. If her fingers on Tristan's arm were any indication, she was more than cold; she was freezing.

Tristan eased an arm around her and cinched her against him. *Bestowing warmth,* he told himself. It was ten shades of wrong to let a woman suffer, especially when he could so easily fix it. Josie conformed herself to him, soaking up the heat like an abandoned kitten. Tristan worked hard to focus on the kitten imagery, not letting himself dwell on her softness, on the way her femininity provided such a nice contrast to his masculinity. The contrast grew stronger when she melded against him, seeking more warmth. His hand eased up and down her arm, chafing, and she gave a little shudder.

"You know what else warms you? Running," Gabe said. He pulled his foot up behind him, stretching. "Are we doing this or what?"

"Don't be jelly," Eli said, also leaning forward to stretch.

"Shut up, Eli," Gabe muttered.

"We're ready," Josie said, easing away from Tristan. The loss of warmth was sudden and chilling for both of them. Tristan almost felt cold, and he was never cold.

They started to jog, an easy pace. "Is this too slow for you?" Josie asked.

"Nah, I like to be able to talk when I run," Tristan replied.

"You don't talk when you're standing still, but you blab while you run?" Eli said. Of the four, he was the most winded. Josie, Tristan noted, kept pace as easily as he did.

"He's complex and deep," Josie said, jabbing Eli's arm.

"Gah, don't touch me when I'm running. I'll tip over and, like a turtle, never rise again," Eli panted. "Hate running so much. Why do I let you guys talk me into this?"

"Cause you love us?" Josie suggested.

"No, it's because I'm a buffer, a big, fat Josie and Gabe buffer," Eli said.

"Eli," Josie said.

"What? The current boyfriend doesn't know about the last one?" Eli said.

"We never went out," Gabe said, but his tone was surly.

"I'm fine with it," Tristan said easily. "Sounds like you've been looking out for her a while."

"We've been friends a long time," Gabe returned. Now he sounded suspicious, like he didn't know where Tristan was going. Josie kept quiet, too, letting the situation play out to Tristan's satisfaction. She had no idea what knowledge or insight he hoped to gain from Gabe and Eli. To her they had always been acquaintances, their friendship resting on shared silliness and the occasional run, minus all the drama with Gabe. It annoyed her to hear him reduce their decade long drama to nothing, but it was as she expected. Gabe used to have her tied up in knots, the way he'd lead her on, flirt with her, kiss her, and then ignore her when something better came along.

"Bart told me how you tuned him in to the bad boyfriend," Tristan said, and Josie almost stumbled.

"You did what?" she said, darting a glance at Gabe. She would have stumbled then, but Tristan reached out a steadying hand, righting her.

"Josie, come on. That guy was trouble."

"Maybe, but you went to Bart behind my back? What else have you colluded with my brother on?"

"Nothing," Gabe said.

"Eh, not exactly true," Eli puffed.

"Stay out of it," Gabe growled.

"You don't think I want to? You two keep dragging me back in," Eli muttered.

"What is he talking about?" Josie demanded.

"Nothing," Gabe said.

Josie stopped and put out a hand, stopping Gabe, too. "Gabe, I've been doing a lot of work to let go of stuff. If you know something that could help me do that, I want to hear what it is. Please."

Tristan paused beside her, his bulk adding more weight to her request.

Gabe glanced between them and then away. "I was worried about the Tony thing, okay? You couldn't or maybe wouldn't see where it was heading, but that guy was an abuser."

"Is that what Eli's talking about?" Josie looked at Eli who stared hard at Gabe.

"No, I'm talking about what happened before. With the guy, the threat."

Josie and Tristan both tensed, eyes boring into Gabe.

"What?" Josie demanded.

"It's just...You and I were kind of talking around then, you know? After prom, we were kind of between. And then I started seeing Katie, and you didn't take it well."

"Okay," Josie drawled. "I was a teenager with a crush. What does this have to do with the other thing?"

"I was pretty sure...I thought...I told Bart..." He paused, took a breath, and let it out. "You were so upset, so mad at me, kind of into the drama of it all. I thought...I thought you made it up to get my attention."

"You thought I made up the worst thing that's ever happened to me for *you*? And you told my brother that?"

"It was ten years ago, Josie," Gabe said. "We were kids."

She crossed her arms. "What was Bart's response?"

"Josie," Gabe said, sighing.

"What?" Josie demanded.

Gabe looked at her, a little sad, a little guilty. "He said he thought you probably were, but to keep it to myself so I didn't embarrass you."

She turned away from Gabe, toward Tristan. Her eyes were teary and she worked hard not to let them overflow. What could she possibly say? That her brother and one of her closest friends thought she was a drama queen who made up a threat and gave a police report for attention? Did the rest of her family think that? The rest of her friends? Did everyone view her that way? A crackpot who would do anything to keep the focus on herself?

Tristan rested his hands on her shoulders. "I know you didn't make it up." His thumbs smoothed over her shoulders, and that was soothing. But it was his simple statement, said with so much conviction, that actually made her feel better. She sniffed and gave a little nod, dashing at her brimming eyes.

"You weren't even there," Gabe said, annoyed.

"Man, you are not helping your cause," Eli murmured.

"Come on, Eli. You can't say you believed her back then. It was crazy," Gabe said, whirling on his friend.

"It was crazy, but Josie's not. She would never make up something like that, be that freaked out and upset, make a statement to the police, not leave her house for two weeks because you chose Katie over her. You've done the same thing to her on repeat multiple times since and she's never made up another threat," Eli said.

That gave Gabe pause. "But...seriously, Josie. A stranger really stopped you in the street and told you he was going to kill you, out of the blue and for no reason."

Josie didn't answer. She was too angry and hurt.

"Just because you don't know his reason doesn't mean he doesn't have one," Tristan said.

"Of course you would say that. You're trying to make a good impression," Gabe said. "But I have been here since we were kids, looking out for her. So, yes, I went to Bart when you were dating an abuser because no one else could see it but me, and I saw the danger signs. And maybe no one else can see this but me, so I am telling you to let it go. Maybe some wacko said something to you, but you turned it into this whole big thing that's taken over your life. No one is coming for you, no one is going to kill you." He'd apparently been saving it up because his tone rose, along with his hand gestures. By the end he was yelling and flailing.

Again Josie turned away from him, toward Tristan. Her brows rose questioningly, silently asking for his take on Gabe's statement. A week ago he would have agreed. But there was something off somewhere and he hadn't identified yet what it was. Until he did that, he couldn't say for certain it was nothing. "I'm not done yet," he told her. "Until then, you keep trusting your gut. No stone unturned, I swear." He tipped forward and kissed her forehead, as if sealing the vow.

Josie drew in a breath and leaned toward him, palms flat on his abs.

"Well, this has been awkward and uncomfortable on all the levels," Eli said, breaking the moment.

With a laugh, Josie eased away from Tristan and squeezed Eli's arm. "Let's go back. I don't think this run can sustain any more drama."

They had come about two miles. They turned and headed back, jogging in silence now. When they reached their cars, Gabe spoke.

"Josie, are we okay?"

Josie regarded him, thinking. "Yep, absolutely."

He frowned, confused by her serenity.

"Josie, are *we* okay?" Eli teased in an obvious effort to lighten the mood.

"No, I hate you," Josie said and jumped on his back, hugging his neck. "But I've always hated you."

"Yes, maintaining the status quo is my lifeblood," Eli said, reaching behind him to pat her head. She gave him a squeeze and hopped off, ignoring Gabe as she reached for her car door, but it was Tristan who put out his hand to halt her.

"Have coffee with me."

She hadn't asked, certain he'd rebuff her again. So it came as something of a surprise for him to make the suggestion. "Okay. Do you want to follow me? I know a place."

"Ride with me," he said, turning toward his car without waiting for her response.

"I guess I'm riding with him," Josie said to Eli and Gabe who were watching the exchange.

"Way to assert your independence, queen," Eli said, tossing her a little salute.

Rolling her eyes, Josie purposely turned her back to him and to Gabe, who watched her through narrowed, suspicious eyes.

CHAPTER 10

Josie scooted into Tristan's car and took a deep breath, inhaling his clean and musky scent.

"Smells like boy," she noted.

"That's because I have a couple of them locked in the trunk," Tristan said, deadpan, and Josie laughed. "You doing okay?"

"Yes," she said, surprised he was asking. "You did try to warn me about the skeletons. I suppose I should have assumed Gabe would be on that list."

"What's the deal with you two? You didn't mention him, in the beginning."

"I didn't want to. Gabe was my fate, or so I used to believe. We were friends with feelings for each other. I think we always kept each other in our back pockets as a someday maybe contingency."

"Is that past tense I hear?" he asked.

"Gabe caused me a lot of hurt, for a long time. We would get close to the line, and then he would get scared and find someone else. It was painful. And then one day it was like I had an epiphany that he only hurt me because I let him. For so many years I thought I had to keep hanging on, taking what he dished out because we were somehow meant for each other. And I realized that's not true. He has zero control over me, over my affections. As soon as I got my mind clear, it was like I'd been cured from some plague. Suddenly he was just Gabe, my pal who happened to be a good kisser. And I sort of lost the desire to ever kiss him again."

"Somehow I don't think he's gotten the memo on your change of heart," Tristan said.

She shrugged. "I don't care. That's the beauty of letting go of that particular emotional attachment. I don't have to be responsible for his thoughts and feelings, only mine. And mine are free. Gabe is a friend, that is all. That's why I didn't mention him because despite our murky past, it's just that: our past. He's my pal and my boss, my occasional running partner, but nothing more."

"But it still hurt you that he contacted Bart."

"It hurts me that my brother believed him over me, but I guess it shouldn't. Bart has never viewed me as anything but an albatross he's been saddled with since my birth." She stared glumly out the window, not actually taking in any of the scenery.

Tristan parked and reached across the console, resting his hand on her knee. "Josie, I'm not the world's most sensitive guy, but I know that's not true. I've rarely seen a brother love his sister more than Bart adores you. And you're missing out on one key possibility here."

She faced him, resting her head on the seat behind her. "What's that?"

"Maybe Gabe is lying."

Her lashes fluttered. "About which part?"

"All of it. Maybe he believed you, maybe he had something to do with the threat, maybe Bart's reaction wasn't what he said. The guy has proved his willingness to trample and manipulate your emotions for the last decade. He accused you of enjoying the drama, but he seems to have thrived on it. How else to explain the times he's led you on and dropped you?"

Her mouth opened and an incredulous little puff of air escaped. "Wow, that's...that's some good and powerful stuff. Do you know that's the first time in my entire life someone has taken my side in the Gabe debacle? I feel like everyone, including him, including my friends and family, has been gaslighting me, telling me we're meant to be and I should get over the hurt he caused me, suggesting that maybe he needs to sew his wild oats before he gives in and decides to be with me, telling me I'm the one he secretly loves while he dates everyone else. Do you know how many times he has kissed me while he's had a girlfriend, and then made it seem like *I'm* the one chasing *him*? When I think about it like that, it makes me so mad."

"Anger steals your joy. Let it go and hold on to the peace you've found. It's not worth it."

She smiled. "Who knew I'd be getting amazing life advice from the private security I hired?"

"You bought the deluxe package," he reminded her.

"I really think I did," she said, reaching over to give his leg a little squeeze. They sat like that, cozy in his warm car while the cool wind whipped around them, hands resting on each other's legs, until the simmering tension between them edged toward a boil. "Can I ask you a question?"

He tensed. "Depends on what it is?"

"What's your last name?"

"Evans."

"That's normal."

"You didn't think it would be?" he said.

"I thought it would be something to fit the persona, like Punchface."

"Tristan Punchface has a nice ring to it. I'll consider, if I ever decide to change."

"I'm trying really hard to clean up my emotional debris, get my life in order. It feels pretty good," she said. "More than that, it feels exciting, like a world of possibility is opening up before me. I already decided I don't have to be captive to Gabe's changes of heart. Now I'm moving past my long-held fear of the threat. What else is out there? It's Josie's time to shine." She used her free hand to make a little flourish and then pressed it to her eyes. "I sound like a lunatic."

"You sound like a woman who is ready to get her life back after having it hijacked by a psycho," Tristan said. "No shame in being enthused."

She dropped her hand and grinned at him. "It's good you think that because 'enthused' is kind of my go-to emotion."

"Me too," he said in his flat, deadpan way and almost smiled when she giggled, shoulders shaking.

"How come you do that?" she asked.

"Make you laugh? I like the sound of it."

"Refuse to laugh or show emotion yourself," she said.

"In my line of work, it's best to leave emotion off the table, gets more results. No one would take me seriously if I giggled through every interview."

"Maybe not, but I'd find it pretty cute. Although I find you pretty cute without the giggling, so…maybe it would be overkill."

He took her hand, giving it a little squeeze. "I'm confused because this feels like flirting, but you promised me glitter and paste, Miss Davis."

"If I thought it would make a dent in that protective shell, maybe I would break out the glitter and paste. Something tells me it wouldn't," she said.

He faced forward but maintained possession of her hand. "Experience is a good teacher. Mine has taught me it's best not to mix business with anything else, namely emotion."

"Can you really control your emotions that well? Enough to cauterize all feelings when you're on a case?"

"Yes," he said.

"Then what's this?" she held up their joined hands.

"This is due to the fact that I think you're pretty cute, too, Josie Davis. But this is as far as I can go while working."

Did he place significant emphasis on "while working" or was that her imagination? Was he trying to say they might have a future after her case was finished? Did she want that? She had no idea. Better to keep things light and friendly than to delve into something she might not want or be ready for. All she knew about him was that he was attractive, not exactly the basis for lifelong love.

"Here's what I know about you: your name is Tristan Evans. You're easy on the eyes, and you might be a felony kidnapper. Care to add anything to the list?" She eyed him, resting her head on the seat behind her.

"I like women who wear toads and flamingos on their sweaters and make their own lozenges," he said.

She laughed out loud. "Your dating life must have been vast and varied."

"I won't bore you with the list; it's endless," he said. They remained staring at each other, holding hands, and it was…nice. Sweet and wholesome and everything Tristan had come to associate with Josie since he met her.

"We still haven't gotten that coffee," she noted.

"Are you still cold?" he asked.

"No, I feel good."

"Maybe we could grab it to go," he suggested, noting the river walk not too far away from the coffee shop.

"That sounds grand."

They ordered their coffee to go, black for him and a peppermint white chocolate mocha for her.

"Want some?" she asked when he eyed it with gimlet suspicion.

He took it, sipped, and handed it back with an expressionless, "Hmm."

"You like?"

"It tastes exactly like you smell, and also probably how you'll taste."

She swallowed a too-big gulp and pressed her hand to her mouth to avoid spewing. "I don't know where to go after that."

"Probably nowhere acceptable. Tell me about your sleep issues."

"Ah, sleep. My arch nemesis. It goes like this: teaching kindergarten takes a lot of energy."

"You have a lot of energy to give," he noted. She was a ball of it, even now as they walked she bounced and used her hands, a mass of quivering kinetic motion.

"I'm well-suited in all the ways. By bedtime I am exhausted. I stumble comically toward the mattress, sometimes not even pausing to put on my jammies."

"Let the record show I am purposely not mocking your use of the word jammies," he inserted.

"Duly noted, thank you. I fall asleep fine and then wake in a panic, convinced he's in the room with me. I have to go through this whole routine, first telling my brain I'm safe, he's not there, he won't find me. Then I have to convince my senses. I don't smell him; I don't hear him; I don't see him. Occasionally I can fall back asleep. Most of the time not. Last month I..." she trailed off, embarrassed.

"What?" he prodded.

"I bought a new body butter and forgot. Then I woke in the night and smelled it and it triggered a full panic attack. That was when I decided to get help."

"What flavor?" he asked.

"My panic attack? Tasted metallic."

"The body butter."

"Pumpkin vanilla."

With a groan, he brought her wrist to his nose and sniffed. "Pumpkin vanilla."

"It's my lifelong dream to be a sexy jack-o-lantern," she said, and he coughed. Automatically she reached into her pocket and pulled out the tin of lozenges. He opened his mouth and she placed one on his tongue.

"That's so much better than handing one over," she noted. "Going to try that with all my friends now."

"I'd rather you didn't," Tristan said.

She tipped her head, studying him, and linked her arm with his. "I suppose I could save it for you. And guess what."

"What?" he asked.

She reached in her pocket and presented him with the glitter glue stick she'd found when she reached for the lozenges. "Consider this official flirtation."

He came the closest he had ever come to smiling, and that was when she realized how much she wanted to break him, to hear him laugh out loud while on the job. Maybe she was evil, because suddenly it was all she could think about. *How can I break this man?* There had to be something wrong with that, didn't there? Even if the intent was only to make him laugh?

"You got quiet," he noted.

"You're always quiet," she returned.

"I'm supposed to be. You." He paused and faced her, touching gentle fingers to the velvet Scrunchie in her ponytail. "You're sparkle and sunshine."

He was so intense, possibly the most intense person she'd ever met. It should have been a warning signal of danger, but instead it worked the opposite, intriguing her and drawing her in. "And do you like sparkle and sunshine?"

"It's becoming vital, like oxygen," he said.

"Pass the glitter glue back, that was definite flirtation," she said.

She almost got him that time, swore she saw his jaw tick with a repressed smile. But then he handed her the glue stick, waiting to continue their walk until she tucked it back into her pocket.

CHAPTER 11

"Can I ask you a question?"

He tensed, and she squeezed his bicep. "You don't have to do that."

"Do what?"

"Freeze like I'm about to ask you to be my live liver donor," she said.

"I don't like to talk about myself," he said.

"You're joking," she said, deadpan, and he put her in a headlock, giving her neck a gentle squeeze.

"Ask your question," he commanded, dropping his arm and taking the final sip of his coffee. He looked for a place to toss the cup, remembered they were in the middle of a bike path, and put his arm down.

"I'm going to assume, based on your job choice, that you've been in some dicey, maybe even scary situations."

He nodded his assent.

"My question is how do you turn off the fear? How are you not afraid? Because I'm tired of being afraid. I don't want to feel fear anymore."

"You can't control fear. It's an automatic response, like blinking or breathing," Tristan said.

"So that's it, I'm doomed."

"Of course not. You can't control feeling afraid, but you can control your response to it. You already do it, when you wake in the night. First you start with your head, and then you work on your other senses."

"Pretend you're talking to one of my kindergarteners and break it down to a molecular level because it doesn't work at night. Why would it work during the day?"

"Because you didn't believe," he said.

"You mean all this time all that was missing was Santa magic?"

"Something like that. You believe it's some innate skill, but really it's a mind game. Train your brain and your body will follow. Practice not being afraid. Create muscle memory with your responses. Don't freeze like an animal with a strong startle reflex. Move. Fight."

"Yes, but you're *you*. Look at you. Of course you're not afraid."

"Do you think I've always looked like this?" he asked, amused.

"Yes, I do. I picture the other children in school fleeing from you in terror, not daring to mess with you."

He coughed and coughed again, this time preemptively reaching for a lozenge before she could offer. She held still as his hand eased into her pocket reaching for the little metal tin.

"Uh, no," he finally said when he tucked it away again. "I've had a lot of training, both mental and physical, to reach the place I am right now. No one is born knowing how to deal with fear. It's a learned behavior that can be learned by everyone."

"Okay, say I agree with you. The things I can learn are far different from the things *you* can learn. I can punch someone all day long and not have it be as effective as a tap from you."

"True," he said, then held up his hands in surrender. "What? I'm agreeing with you. But you're still missing the point. No, you can't destroy someone with a punch. But you're not helpless. You can scream, you can run, you can fight back. You can carry a gun. But your biggest weapon by far is the fact that you can control your fear.

You don't have to be held hostage to it, you just have to practice, to train your mind, to master your responses."

"Huh," she said, thinking.

They walked in companionable silence for a while, making a circle that brought them back to his truck. "I was thinking about what you said, about practicing not being afraid."

"Why do I have a foreboding feeling?" he said.

"Because apparently you're perceptive. My friends want to have one last hurrah before Jenna has her baby."

"I'm terrified to know how this involves me."

"They want to go clubbing."

He tossed her a look. "That hugely pregnant woman I saw wants to go clubbing?"

"It might be her last time for the rest of her life," Josie said, tone impassioned. "And they want me to go, which would be my first time ever, because I've always been too afraid."

"I can't picture you at a club."

"Maybe you could, if you saw it in person."

His brows rose. "You want me to go clubbing with you?"

"I wouldn't be afraid if you were there."

"Isn't the point of you going to overcome your fear on your own?"

She jutted a finger at him. "You never said it had to be on my own. Getting a taste of it, seeing it's not so scary with you beside me might get the ball rolling, encourage me to do other things I find scary."

"Like what other things?" he asked.

"Basically anything beyond breathing."

He tossed her another look. "It sounds kind of like a date type situation."

"Does it? I didn't mean for it to. I just want a beefy male companion to… Okay, I hear it now, and it's tanking. But it's not a date, don't think of it that way. Think of it as a work outing, a special detail. You're providing security for me at my event."

"Your *event*," he said, biting his cheek hard to avoid giving in to the smile that wanted to blossom. For the life of him he couldn't fathom Josie at a club. She was far too wholesome.

"Yes, I will be Club Girl, complete with my own bouncer in tow."

He stopped at a light and turned to study her, cute bouncy pony-tail, ink-stained fingers from too many hits with markers, her makeup-free visage making her look about eighteen. "I suppose that would be okay," he said with a passing imitation of reluctance. In reality it would take a stick of dynamite to keep him away.

Josie sighed when they reached her car, and it took Tristan a minute to understand why. Gabe sat on her hood, waiting impatiently.

"I could tell him to leave," Tristan offered. "I could take you straight home."

"No, he probably wants to make sure we're okay, after the Bart revelation. It'll be fine. It's just Gabe."

Josie watched Gabe, and Tristan watched her. He didn't like the Gabe situation, but he couldn't tell if it was because something was truly off or, more embarrassingly, because he was jealous. *This is why feelings should never interfere with the job.* Everything became too muddled. Still, Gabe thought they were dating. He would never kick someone he was dating out of his truck and drive away. So he parked, got out, and walked Josie to her car, taking satisfaction in how much the proprietary action bothered Gabe. Gabe seemed to believe he had some claim on Josie, despite the fact that they had never officially dated. That assumption of Josie's loyalty had bound her to him for a time, but had hurt her deeply. How was he so obtuse to the pain he'd brought her? Or, worse, did he thrive on that pain? Enjoy the ego boost it gave him? An honorable man would not, and that was the thing Tristan couldn't discern. Was Gabe honorable or a weasel?

They came to a halt in front of Josie's car, Gabe scowling between them.

"Josie, I wanted to talk to you," Gabe said pointedly. Between the imperious tone and his kinglike sprawl on Josie's vehicle, it was hard to see him as anything but nefarious at the moment.

"Tristan was dropping me," Josie said unnecessarily, pressing her hand to his bicep. Whether she was actually drawing strength or that was only his imagination, he also didn't know. In any case he leaned close, resting his hand on her waist as he whispered in her ear, blocking Gabe's presence entirely.

"Don't let him gaslight you; you've got this. You are strong and brave."

Her answering smile was so sweet, so *thankful*, it went all the way to his soul. Had no one ever said those things to her before? Had no one ever believed in her? Because that was how it felt to Tristan, and he didn't like it.

"Have a good day," she said, which was such a Josie thing to say he had to bite the inside of his cheek again. She noticed the cheek tick and squeezed his bicep, shaking her head a little.

He squeezed her waist, where his hand still rested, and went to his truck without a glance or goodbye to Gabe.

"Bye," Gabe called loudly and obviously, tossing him an obnoxious wave.

"Gabe," Josie said, wearily, purposely not watching Tristan drive away. She didn't know why the thought should make her feel small and helpless, but it did. With him, she felt powerful and brave. Without him she was once again the same old Josie, scared of her own shadow.

"What are you doing with that guy?" Gabe demanded, whirling on her. "He is so not your type."

"How do you know what my type is?" She climbed on the hood beside him and sat down. It felt like high school, going to the airport at night to watch the planes arrive and depart. That had been a prime makeout spot. She and Gabe went twice, made out both times, and both times he followed it up by a purposeful denouncement of their relationship. *Come on, Josie, let's not ruin our friendship. It was just for fun.* Had he known she hadn't viewed it that way? Had he realized she wasn't casual about her kisses? If not, it made him obtuse. If so, it made him something much worse, almost a predator.

He puffed a derisive little laugh, full of too much cockiness for her tastes.

Usually Josie was content to follow his lead and let him set the tone for their relationship, but all of a sudden she couldn't take it any longer. "I don't understand you, Gabe. You say you want to be friends, and then you don't act like one."

"What, you think I'm jealous? Of that guy?" He pointed in the direction Tristan had left.

"I don't know what you are," Josie said.

"I'm a concerned friend. That guy will only end in heartbreak."

"Why?" Josie asked.

"Because he's like a robot. He's so mechanical. I didn't view one facial expression from him except glacial. And you are all soft and warm. That guy isn't you. He'll hurt you."

Josie let that lay for a minute, thinking. On the surface of things it sounded good. He was being a concerned friend. He saw that she and Tristan were different types and worried. But it only took a little bit of digging to come up with the truth.

"Tristan is a new friend, and we're different. But in the short time I've known him, he's given me more insight and confidence in myself than anyone I've ever met." The way Tristan looked at her, the things he said to her. It was like he believed she was special and capable, and it made her believe those things, too. Not like Gabe who always made her feel like she was too much. That she was being too much, asking too much, assuming too much.

Gabe puffed another laugh and shook his head. "Just because some built meathead pays you a little attention does not mean he's potential husband material. Guys like that never stick around."

Josie bristled. "I never said I wanted him to be husband material, and I never asked him to stick around. I'm not some psycho who starts making wedding plans with every guy I meet."

"Just guys you've known forever," he said, aiming for a joke and failing mightily. He grinned at her, but the barb was too sharp and struck too deep.

"You think I'm in love with you," she blurted, saying the words out loud she'd never dared.

"Aren't you?" he returned, dead serious.

She stared at him, gobsmacked by his overt self-assurance. "No, I am not," she said at last. "Maybe there was a time when I might have been close, when a little reassurance or affection from you might have tipped me over the edge. But what I am instead is wary and cautious and self-protective because *you* have made me that way. You have led me on and dropped me so many times I feel like I bounce. And, clearly unknown to you, I hopped off the carousel a while back. Let me officially tell you, so we're both clear, I view you as a friend and nothing more. I haven't seen you that way in a long time, in years."

"Okay," he said, but his tone and wry smile told her he didn't believe her. There was a part of Josie that wanted to argue, to try and drive home her point. But she also realized that the more impassioned she became in her assertion, the less believable it became. All she could do was let it go, and there was a certain power in that, in not caring that he believed she clung pathetically to the scraps he tossed her. The only challenge, in her mind, was whether their friendship could survive his ego. Maybe she didn't want it to, and that was a chilling thought. Josie wasn't the sort of person who let go of people, as proved by the fact that she'd had the same friends since middle school. But things with Gabe weren't working, had possibly become toxic. At what point was it okay to give up on someone and move on?

She didn't think she was there yet, but the fact that she allowed herself the possibility was a step forward. She took a deep breath and let it out, consciously releasing her annoyance. "Gabe, despite what you believe, I only want the best for you. I want you to be happy."

"Same, Jo-Jo," Gabe said, regaining his former good cheer. He hopped off her hood and dusted his pants, adding, "And it's not with that guy."

As he got in his car and drove away, Josie realized they hadn't mentioned Bart or Gabe's betrayal, his disbelief of her story. She had been waiting for him to apologize and he had instead bamboozled her into talking about *him*, about their relationship and her feelings. *How does he do that to me?* she wondered, shaking her head as she slid off the hood. Even though she felt good about holding her own in the conversation, she was annoyed that she had let him divert her from her original intent, from discussing how he had run to her brother like a tattletale, telling on her for her relationship with Tony and his disbelief over the threat. She couldn't help but wonder if he would do the same now. Would he fly to Bart and express his concerns over Tristan?

On the other hand she took a step toward being brave, toward addressing the elephant in the room with Gabe, AKA his unwavering belief in her adoration. She had skirted the issue for too long. Setting the record straight today—even if he didn't believe her—was a huge adrenaline rush. She pulled out her phone, wavered in indecision for a few seconds, and decided to go for it.

I was brave.

Tristan replied immediately, as if he'd been waiting. *I am proud.*

For the rest of the day, Josie felt a little glow nothing else could dim.

CHAPTER 12

Tristan hadn't been clubbing in years, more than a decade at least. When he was a kid it had seemed like good fun. Since becoming an adult he learned too much about the seedy underbelly of most clubs. By far there were too many fights, assaults, rapes, and drugs for his tastes. But he also admitted some were better than others. Certain clubs tended to cater to those with sleazier tastes. The one Josie's friends chose seemed more upper crust and self-respecting. A good place to go for dancing, light cocktails, and mingling. Given that one of their crew was nine months pregnant, it was probably their safest bet in town. Still, it set his instincts tingling as he arrived at the club and waited for Josie and her friends. So many dark corners, blind alleys, and hidden exits. The place had the potential to be a predator's buffet. He was glad he was there, if only to keep Josie safe, especially because she had never been to a club before. Though he would never tell her, he hoped she would get her fill after this and never go again.

Josie and her friends weren't hard to spot as they ascended the crowded street. One of them was hugely pregnant and waddled. Collectively they were years older than the average twenty something by the door, and then there was Josie, at the center of the group, smiling as one of her friends talked with animated hand motions.

They saw Tristan as a unit and paused in front of him as if depositing Josie on his doorstep. He scanned her up and down, biting his cheek so hard to stop the smile he swore he tasted blood.

"This is what you wear to a club?" he said.

She glanced down at her feet, assessing. "Not good?"

He hated the waver of insecurity in her tone because he hadn't meant to place it there. She wore one of her ubiquitous sweater and skirt combos, only this time she had added knee-high socks and black combat boots, along with a black velvet beret, complete with a jaunty black feather.

"It's perfect, I love it," he said sincerely.

She glanced at her feet again, blushing this time. "I wasn't sure about the combat boots, but Jenna said they looked tough."

Tristan glanced at Jenna, whose French manicured fingers supported her distended baby belly.

"If anyone knows tough, it's Jenna," Tristan declared, which caused Josie to giggle, shoulders shaking, which caused him to bite his cheek again. At this rate he was going to scar.

"Let's do this thing," Jenna said. She took a step and winced, pausing with her hand on her belly.

"She's not actually in labor, is she?" Tristan asked Josie in a whispered aside as he fell in step beside her.

"No, apparently she's reached that stage where the ligaments pull painfully if she moves a certain way. Pregnancy seems fun." She gave him a sarcastic thumb's up but, despite that, he knew she was lying. She would love being pregnant; she gave off future mom vibes in spades.

He leaned close to whisper in her ear. "On a scale of one to ten, how jealous are you that it's her and not you?"

She blinked, shocked by his perception, and then smiled sheepishly, leaning close to whisper in return. "A hundred and twelve percent."

"You're a math genius," he added, watching the pink stain her cheeks as she eased away and smiled, in amusement this time. She tucked her hand in his and it was…nice. A little bit of belonging in a loud, crowded room where no one seemed to belong to anyone. Already the innocuous bass reverberated through his brain, like a signal that he was past his thirtieth birthday and therefore shouldn't legally be allowed inside a club.

They edged into the crowded club, separating from her friends as they were sucked into the vortex of moving bodies. Josie seemed content to observe for the moment, lip tucked between her teeth as she took it all in with wide eyes.

"What do you think?" he asked, watching her instead of the crowd.

"It's like those old illustrated bible scenes where they depict pre-flood levels of depravity," Josie said.

Tristan turned his attention to the club. A few people had paired off and were grinding, bodies flailing, hands invisible behind clothes, shirts unbuttoned. Beyond that it was fairly tame, comparatively speaking. No one was visibly wasted, falling down, spoiling for a fight, snorting or shooting drugs.

"It's not so bad," Tristan soothed.

"I must sound like an idiot to you," she noted.

"What? Of course you don't. Why would I think that?"

"Because you've seen so much more than I have."

"In what universe would that be a good thing?"

Her mouth opened, but no words came out.

He shifted closer, trying to talk over the thrumming base without screaming. "For the record, I don't equate innocence with ignorance. Wholesomeness makes an endearing change of pace."

"Endearing?" she echoed, peering up at him as she tried to read him.

Tristan made certain she could read nothing; it was his specialty. "So endearing," he said, deadpan.

"Endearing enough to dance, maybe?" she asked, giving his hand a squeeze.

"Like that?" he asked, using his head to nod toward the flailing couples on the dance floor.

Her tongue popped out in an automatic gag. "Uh, no. I don't want to lose my feather." She touched the tip of her feather.

Tristan coughed and then coughed again, trying to get himself back under control. "That's the only reason you don't want to grind? For the sake of your feather?"

"If you're using 'feather' as a euphemism for dignity, then yes, for the sake of my feather."

He coughed again, opening his mouth on autopilot when she reached for a lozenge. The song switched, providing them a good opportunity to ease onto the dance floor. It was a fast number and Josie's friends found them, claiming her into their scrum.

When she finally emerged enough to realize Tristan was no longer beside her, her head whipped around searching for him. He stood at the edge of the room, watching, looking wary and large, like the bouncer she'd accused him of being. She caught his eye and crooked her finger at him. He left his post against the wall and walked toward her, the press of bodies parting automatically like he was Moses and they were the Red Sea.

"You disappeared," she accused.

"You were having fun; that was the goal," he reasoned.

"Stay and have fun with me," she said, clutching his hand and giving it a little shake.

A new song started, something mindless and thrumming. She started to sway, and he started to jump.

She laughed. "This is you dancing? Just jumping?"

"No, but there are too many people for the complete display. It's epic."

He said it in his usual deadpan way, but somehow she thought he was serious this time. He had that sort of physical presence and way of moving that said he'd be good at dancing, able to control his body and make it do what he wanted, as proved by the fact that he'd been jumping for a while now and showed no signs of slowing or tiring.

The song switched to a rare slow number. There weren't many of those, given how many people were there for hard and fast dancing. But about every ten songs they threw in something for the couples—

or those people trying to become couples. Tristan and Josie froze, staring at each other. He was so unreadable. She had no idea if he wanted to dance with her. Then he put his hand on her waist, tugging her a little bit closer. She rested a hand on his chest. He added his other hand to the opposite side of her waist. She pressed closer, and they started to sway gently. Her hand shifted to his shoulder, and he swayed her harder, tipping her backwards before pulling her upright again.

"I'm having a very Patrick Swayze moment here," she said.

"Nobody puts Josie in a corner," he said. One of his hands slid to her neck. The eye contact was unbroken and intense, and then the music switched to another fast song, the throb moving faster than their hearts, making them feel out of rhythm. Tristan tilted Josie upright.

"Want to get some air?" he asked.

She nodded, letting him take the lead and make room as he led her outside. They rounded the corner and leaned against the bricks, breathing deep.

"What's your first impression of clubbing?" he asked, being careful to keep his tone neutral.

"Not as scary as I always thought. Not as exciting, either. A little sad, actually." She stared across the alley, eyes on the brick of the wall opposite.

"Sad how?" he asked, mimicking her pose, eyes on the bricks instead of her.

"I'm sure there are other people in there like us, who are here to dance and have fun. But it also seems like there's a lot of desperation, people here because they think they're supposed to be here, and not because they want to be. Like they think being twenty and living life to the fullest equals dancing at a club with strangers. It's almost like they've never experienced the joy of reading a book on a Friday night."

"Sounds like me, at twenty."

It was the most he'd ever revealed about himself. "But not you now?" She turned to look at him.

He faced her, too. "Not me now."

"What changed?" she asked.

He touched a finger to her feather. "Absolutely everything."

Josie wanted to press him for more, to try to get him to open up. The problem was her too-soft heart. The same fear that made her unable to take a chance or leave her house made her fall too hard and too fast, leading to eventual heartbreak. She wanted to believe in others' good intentions. Instead of becoming cynical when she couldn't find them, she retreated, withdrawing into herself, saying she was too busy or too happy to date. The reality was that it all came back to fear, the same fear she'd felt every day of the last decade. Was it even living if she wasn't willing to take a chance?

"You can talk to me, you can tell me things," she tried. It was as far as she was willing to put herself on the emotional tether. "I'm a good listener, I think. I hope."

Tristan drew in a deep breath, tipping forward and inhaling in a way that made her think he was trying to catch her scent. Finally he let it out and said, "Josie." It was only one word, her name, but it was a lot. She didn't think anyone had ever looked at her that way, with so much intensity and desire. That someone like him should want someone like her was laughable to the point of making her uncertain. Was she reading him wrong? Was he this way with every woman? Was she one of an endless stream to him? How else to explain it?

Be brave, she urged herself, taking a tiny step closer. Tristan's gaze turned wary, but he didn't take a step back, didn't push her away. They were very close now, toe to toe, sharing the same invisible circle against the wall. She pressed her palms on his too-good-to-be-true abs and tipped forward slowly, giving him plenty of advance notice and time to stop her. Instead his hand slid to her neck, cupping her face, encouraging her advance without prodding it along. Slowly, slowly, *slowly* she made the long journey from her height to his, heading for his lips. He closed his eyes and drew in a breath.

"There you guys are," one of her friends declared, her voice drunk on adventure and daring.

Tristan and Josie froze, eyes on each other. She eased off of her toes and away; he dropped his hand. "Here we are," she agreed.

"Jenna is having a little too much fun and we had to drag her away for the sake of the baby, so it's not born at a club," Ellie said. "You coming with us, Jo-Jo, or is Tristan going to drop you?" The teasing in her tone was unmistakable. All of her female friends were definitely on the pro-Tristan train, mostly because they believed it was some kind of blip away from real life and Josie's usual type.

"I'm coming," Josie declared, eyes on Tristan, waiting for him to disagree.

He didn't. She gave him a smile and patted his arm, letting him know the air between them was clear.

"I'll touch base in a couple of days, after I look into my next lead. We probably need to have a conversation," he said.

"I thought that's the girl's line, 'We need to talk.'"

"Don't be sexist; boys can be emotionally distant and complex, too," he said, touching a finger to her nose.

Josie laughed. "Story of my life, Tristan. You take care."

"Wait." Tristan halted her, reached in her pocket, and pulled out the tin of lozenges. "One more for the road, to feed my addiction."

Josie watched him with a smile, heart thudding, aware he knew exactly what he was doing to her. The only question, in her mind, was what she was doing to him.

CHAPTER 13

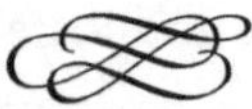

"Need some advice." After pondering the situation a couple of days, Tristan realized he could ask his boss, alleviating a huge weight from his shoulders.

"What's up?" Ribs asked, indicating the open chair across from his desk.

Tristan sat and started with no preamble or small talk. "Josie doesn't want her family to know I'm investigating, but I don't know how else to find the dad's former mistress without letting him know why I'm asking."

Ribs gave a little chuckle and adjusted the picture on his desk. "You're clearly not married. Don't ask the dad; find the wife's friends and ask them. Bonus points: they'll let you know if they still think he's cheating."

"The wife's friends," Tristan breathed. They would be the perfect workaround. "Thanks." He started to stand, but Ribs hailed him back.

"How's it going with Josie? You two working out okay?"

"Yep." Tristan said.

Ribs studied him, probably seeing more than Tristan wanted him to. "Okay. You finding any leads?"

"Not leads, specifically, but some threads. Family and friend relationship situations I'm not happy with. Can't say I think any of that had to do with the threat, but it's enough to keep the book open. Not ready to shut it until I follow up."

"Sounds good. Need any tech support?"

"Not for the moment." He still hadn't had any nibbles on his online posts, more than the usual nutcrackers and people who wanted to argue for no reason.

"This is the perfect case," Ribs said. "Easy work and low overhead. May they all be so simple." He pressed his palms together in a prayerful gesture.

Tristan gave him a little nod. It was easy work and low overhead, but he wasn't certain it was simple, not if his ever increasingly complex feelings toward Josie were any indication. He let himself out of the office and went to stalk Josie's mother's place of work. Unlike her father, who found new work after the affair, her mother had worked at the same place for nearly thirty years, a firm that handled document disposal for sensitive information. That in itself had struck Tristan as odd. What if Josie's threat had something to do with information her mother's company handled? Intriguing as the thought was, he couldn't make the leap. Her mother was an account executive, in charge of procuring the companies whose documents they shredded; she didn't actually handle any classified information. There would be no reason for any of her clients to threaten her children, and especially not Josie specifically.

He parked outside the company and waited for lunch. Knowing he might not get an answer, he texted Josie anyway. *Does your mom eat out for lunch?*

To his surprise, she texted back immediately. *Only on special occasions. This is so fun. Like spies!*

He allowed himself a smile, because no one was around to see it. It felt as indulgent and decadent as he feared, unnatural and freakish on his face. He realized, not for the first time, how little he'd had to smile over lately. Josie was definitely a reason. He could picture her now, up to her knees in kindergarteners and their chaos. *Technically I am a spy at the moment. Peeping on your mom's company.*

That is both creepy and exhilarating, she returned.

Ironically both my senior superlatives in school, he said and smiled again, picturing her laughing.

Yearbook photo or it didn't happen.

There was a tragic...accident. Yearbook burned.

How...convenient. Eep, gotta go. Literal running with scissors going on here.

Tristan stared at his phone, tracing his finger over the words like a lovesick teenager until lunchtime, when the doors of the company opened and people began to flood out. One group of women walked in a pod toward a restaurant at the end of the block. Tristan got out of his car and followed them, keeping a safe distance until they reached the restaurant. He took a breath and purposely softened his features before he reached for the door. It took a lot of effort, a depressing and shocking amount to try and crack his façade and remember who he used to be. He took a determined step inside.

The restaurant was suddenly crowded, overwhelmed with the lunch rush. Tristan eased closer to the group of women, hovering without making it look like he was hovering, waiting and hoping for an opening.

He found it when one of them mentioned the name of their company and allowed himself to do an obvious double take. They paused and looked at him.

"Sorry," he said, aiming for sheepish. "I didn't mean to eavesdrop." *Big fat lie.* "I heard the name *Bellcorp* and I've been sitting across the street staring at the building all day. I wasn't sure someone actually said it or I imagined it."

"You've been staring at our building?" one of the women said. They were homogenously middle aged and plumpish, setting Tristan at ease. He was glad to play on their maternal instincts and not have to try and bluff his way through being flirty.

"Yeah, but saying that out loud sounds pathetic, which is accurate, considering I am pathetic." He swiped his hand over his face, hand scraping on five o'clock shadow that insisted on showing up about six hours early.

"Can we help you with something?" another of the women said.

Tristan dropped his hand, hoping he looked as chagrined as he felt. It was easier to work solo than it was for him to depend on other people. "Well, there's this girl."

One of the women smiled. "Isn't there always? Does she work at *Bellcorp?*"

"No, that's what's dumb. Her mom does. I met her parents, and I'm not sure I made a good impression. I've been sitting in my car wondering if I should make contact, bring flowers, something." He gave a helpless shrug.

"Who's the woman?" one of them asked.

"Marlene Davis."

Collectively, their smiles softened. "Oh, Marlene is the sweetest. Don't worry about her, I'm sure she loved you."

"I don't know. I'm not usually this insecure, but this girl is different, has me tied up in knots. It was like..."

The waitress came to retrieve the group of women and Tristan paused. He felt they were properly vested in his story, a fact confirmed when they invited him to sit with them and keep talking.

"Now, you were telling us about the girl, Marlene's daughter," one of the women said.

"Right. Well, the thing is that I'm new to town, just moved here for a job. I don't know a lot of people, so I kind of lack perspective. Maybe that's why I've gone kind of crazy for this girl."

"Maybe you're just crazy for this girl," another woman said. They were all smiling in that motherly way and Tristan thought he was getting a little too into character because it was comforting, that smile.

"Maybe," he said. "She's something special. I don't want to screw it up, not least of which by making a bad impression on her family."

"But Marlene is so sweet," another woman insisted.

"Have you known her long?" Tristan asked.

The woman waved her hand. "Forever. We don't get a lot of turnover. It's a good place to work. We all tend to be lifers."

Tristan sipped his water, nodding. "I felt like *maybe* I did okay with the mom, but the dad…there was a vibe there. Maybe it's a father/daughter thing?"

The women darted each other looks.

Bingo, Tristan thought. If those looks were any indication, they were dying to spill what they knew about Josie's dad.

"I mean, I've met Ed a few times, and he can be a little reserved," one of the women said.

"This was more than that. It was like I'd stumbled into a conversation already taking place, you know? It was weird, I couldn't put my finger on it," Tristan said, shaking his head as if trying to push off something unpleasant. He let it lay, hoping one of them would pick up the thread.

"Well," one of them drawled, playing with her silverware. "It might not have been about you. They've had some trouble, in the past."

"Oh," Tristan said softly.

Another of the women looked like she was bursting at the seams. She glanced around the group—for permission?—then started to talk. "He had an affair. Like, not a one night thing. A big, two-year relationship. We all thought that was the end. Marlene is usually a total professional, but she was a wreck. I can't count how many times she came to work sobbing and had to leave. I swear more than once I smelled alcohol on her breath."

One of the women hissed. Apparently that was a step too far.

"Oh," Tristan drawled again. "That's the worst. I'm so sorry to hear that. But apparently they worked through it?"

The women nodded. "It was rough, though. Seriously bad."

He toyed with his silverware. "Is it…are you sure it's over? Maybe that was the weird vibe."

"Oh, it's over," one of the women said and the others nodded.

"How do you know?" Tristan asked.

"Because the mistress is dead." The woman who spoke slit a finger across her throat. Tristan's jaw dropped, a real reaction he didn't have to prompt.

"What happened to her?" he asked.

The gossipy woman, the one who had blurted the part about the alcohol, leaned forward to make her next salacious proclamation. "Suicide."

"Oh, wow. That's a lot, that's heavy," Tristan said.

Another woman shrugged. "Solved a lot of problems."

"Not for her husband," another woman said.

"She was married, too?" Tristan asked.

"Yeah. Marlene took it bad, but Yasmin's husband, wow."

"You called her by name. Did you know her?" Tristan asked.

"No, I just learned the whole miserable story. At first Marlene tried to keep it to herself, and then when it was too much she started spilling everything. Her name was Yasmin Parker, she worked with Ed. He ended things, and Yasmin killed herself."

"Wow," Tristan repeated. "That's…wow. Sounds like it was a good thing Marlene had you guys to fall back on."

"We tried to do the best we could. It was a huge mess, but it was also a long time ago. I know she and Ed have been trying hard to repair their relationship since then, and things have seemingly been going well." She paused. "They had some trouble with their kids."

Tristan tensed. "What sort of trouble?"

"Some mental health stuff," one of them said, waving dismissively. "Normal teen stuff, you know?"

When she didn't elaborate, Tristan was wondering which teen she meant. Surely Josie's breakdown after the threat could have been deemed mental health stuff, especially if her family believed she was making it up. Was there more? Something involving Bart or Janine?

The conversation shifted to normal coworker stuff, gossip about other people besides Marlene. Tristan tried to listen and nod politely, but his mind whirred with the new information. Josie's father's mistress committed suicide. What kind of impact did that have on the mistress's family? On Josie's family? Had her husband been upset enough to track Josie down and make threats?

That question should be easy enough to answer.

Lunch finished and Tristan thanked the group for the listening ear and advice. "Hey," one of the women said, laying a motherly hand on his arm. "Let me tell you something. If you really like this girl, if you really think she's worth it, then you do whatever it takes to make it work. Life is hard. Loving someone and being loved in return makes it better."

Tristan nodded, feeling like he'd just been handed the best piece of life advice he'd ever received.

CHAPTER 14

Tracking down the spouse of Yasmin Parker was a piece of cake, thanks to her unusual name. There was only one obituary with that name during the timeframe of Ed Davis's affair. Even more fortuitous for Tristan, Yasmin's husband had a distinct name, too: Eugene. While there were a few Eugene Parkers in the Metro area, it only took a bit of searching before Tristan found the correct one.

He sat outside and observed the house a while, getting a feel for things, trying to figure out how to play it. Bombastic and intimidating? Should he use his size and reserve to demand answers? As he waited the answer presented itself when a man emerged from the house and began weeding. Tristan wanted to resolve the case, but not enough to bully an old man with a garden trowel.

The man looked up when he approached, squinting and shading his eyes. "Mr. Parker?" Tristan said.

"Yes," the man said, tone wary.

Tristan crouched so they were on the same height and he was less intimidating. "I'm looking for the Eugene Parker who was married to Yasmin."

"That's me," the man said, wariness tipping to weariness. "What's this about?"

"I'm afraid it's rather painful and sensitive," Tristan said.

"Sounds about right for Yasmin," he said, returning his attention to his garden.

"She had an affair before she died," Tristan began.

The man laughed bitterly. "Which one?"

"She had more than one affair?"

Eugene paused and stared at the house. "Have you ever known a woman who couldn't seem to survive without drama? That was Yasmin, and that was something I learned after she was already pregnant and we were married. She thrived on pitting people against each other, on fueling animosity and discord. Never had a peaceful moment in our lives until she was dead." He struck his trowel in the ground with a hard shove.

"I'm here specifically in regard to Ed Davis."

"Oh, that one." His tone held no animosity, only an ancient sort of exhaustion at once again having to deal with something he'd probably dealt with a lot. "He lasted longer than most. The only thing I could figure was that he was the calm sort who became fascinated by the drama. Other dramatic ones were flashes in the pan."

"Forgive me if I'm overstepping here, but you sound fairly okay with the fact that your wife was seeing other men."

He gave a harsh chuckle and shook his head. "Okay? Try dead. When Yasmin and I were first married, I thought we were soul mates, true love and all that. The first time she took a lover I lost my mind, threatened to kill him, her, myself. The second time, I was less shocked. By the third time I realized it was a pattern, one intended to get my reaction. So I stopped having them."

"Why didn't you divorce?" Tristan asked.

He shrugged. "Divorce takes as much energy as being married, in some cases. We had children, we'd still share them if we split up. Financially it was better to stay together, and in other ways, too. We were settled, had a good division of labor. She may have slept around, but she kept the house clean and the meals prepared. It was cheaper than hiring a housekeeper, so long as I dampened any emotional investment."

"About a decade ago, someone threatened Ed Davis's daughter, said he was going to track her down and kill her."

Eugene paused, brow crinkling. "Did he? Is she dead?"

"No," Tristan drawled. "Do you know anything about it?"

"Not a thing."

"It was a strange reaction you just had," Tristan said.

"When you spend much of your life in an emotional overdraft, it sort of empties the account. None of my reactions are normal to anything anymore, none of my feelings, either. I try to put up a front for my kids but, to tell the truth, I don't have much to give. I suppose what you're asking is if I had anything to do with that threat, that girl. The answer is no. I had nothing but pity for Ed Davis and anyone stupid enough to become involved with Yasmin. Since her death, I've done my best to put the past behind me with no need to ever revisit it again, either with sadness or vengeance. I can only hope he was able to move on and put the pieces of his life back together better than I was."

Tristan believed him. On the other hand, "You have children."

Eugene gave another humorless chuckle. "Barking up the wrong tree there. Somehow, despite how badly we botched it, our kids turned out good. They're settled, happy, married with kids and living their lives. I have no idea how, but they're doing okay. Not exactly filled with craziness and hatred like they have a right to be."

Fathers could be biased about their children, but somehow he didn't think Eugene was. He seemed genuinely shocked that his children were doing well. Tristan would look into them, but he felt he'd reached a dead end, possibly his last.

"Thank you for your time, sir. I'm sorry to bring up painful memories."

"You didn't," Eugene said, tone placid as he kept his eyes on his plants.

Tristan waited until he was away from the house to text Josie.

We need to have that conversation.

Supper tonight?

Probably best if it's not in public, he reluctantly told her, knowing it would increase her anxiety.

My place? I'll cook.

Can I bring anything? he offered.

A wink and a smile, she replied and he allowed himself to smile at his phone. Could he give her that much of himself? He honestly didn't know. Hopefully by the time he saw her in person, he would have it figured out.

"You are predictably and painfully prompt," Josie said when she answered the door.

She wore one of her ubiquitous dresses, sans sweater. Instead it was topped by, "An apron," Tristan groaned.

Josie looked down, inspecting herself. "You don't like aprons?"

"As of this moment, I love them," Tristan said earnestly.

Blushing, she moved aside to let him enter. He did so, inhaling deeply. "I've come to associate good smells with you."

"That's weird, but better than the alternative, I suppose."

"How can I help?" he asked.

"Do you cook?" she returned.

"No, but I'm pretty good at following orders," he said.

"Are you?" she asked, tipping to look at him.

"When I trust my commander," he said, touching a finger to her shoulder. "Lead, Josie, and I will follow."

"Wow, that casual statement deserves a lot more pondering than I have time for. But I'm actually ready, just waiting for the lasagna to finish cooking."

"Lasagna," Tristan said.

"You say a lot of words in that reverential tone," Josie noted.

"Only lately," Tristan returned. They arrived in her kitchen and he did a slow scan. "Yellow."

"Step one: give him the colorblind test. Check."

"Step one: affirm notion that cheerful girl has a cheerful kitchen. Check."

"You think I'm cheerful?" she said.

"You don't?" he said.

"I think of myself more as a quivering mass of anxiety," she said.

"And that doesn't cheer you?" he said in his deadpan way that somehow made her laugh harder.

"Speaking of anxiety," she said, steering the conversation to its ultimate purpose. Tristan didn't want to get into it yet and felt relieved when the timer dinged.

"It's like you planned that," she said as she reached for her oven mitts and opened the oven door. Heat and garlic streamed out, making Tristan's mouth water. Josie set the picture-perfect lasagna on the counter between them and they stared at it in silence a minute, enjoying the sensory overload. "I almost hate to cut it when it turns out this well. It doesn't always."

"Your failures are undoubtedly a thousand times better than my successes. This looks and smells amazing."

Pleased, she turned to the refrigerator for the salad and directed him to the cupboard to reach for plates.

"It's nice to have someone tall to retrieve those. Usually it's a balancing act on my tiptoes that makes me feel like I'm about to crash and burn and obliterate all my dinnerware."

"Why do you put them so high?" he asked.

She paused as if she'd never considered before. "I don't know. I guess because that's where my mom keeps them in her house. But I don't have to keep them in the same place. I can keep them wherever I want. You're blowing my mind here, Evans."

"It was my turn, Davis," he said. He set aside the plates and reached for the glasses.

"Wow, are you always so good with the words and the flirting?"

"No," he said.

"Not going to elaborate?"

"No."

She blew out a breath. He passed behind her and squeezed her hip, a gentle little teasing gesture that did nothing to ease her annoyance.

Supper did, however. By the time they sat at the table, she seemed content to make pleasant and easy small talk. Tristan was a little stunned by her ability to find innocuous subjects they could both talk about. Small talk was a skill he had never possessed. Sometimes it annoyed him when people chattered banally, but with Josie he took it as the gift it was. She was astute enough to realize he didn't want to talk about anything deep for the moment. They would get to her difficult conversation later. As for the stuff about him, hopefully never.

He helped her clean up, drying dishes while she washed. It was a cozy and domestic little scene that went straight to his heart and lingered and he had a hard time taking his eyes off her. Either she was playing ignorant on purpose, or she was too intent on her thoughts because she didn't seem to notice. Finally she drained the water in the sink, dried her hands, and faced him.

"Now?"

"Now," he agreed with a nod. He led the way to the couch. Josie tucked her hand in his as if she needed the moral support. He gave it an encouraging squeeze. This was not going to be easy, and he dreaded it. But more than that he dreaded living with the weight of secrets it would cause between them.

They sat on her couch, probably a hand me down because it was a little worn and lumpy. In Josie style, she had added a plethora of colorful quilts and pillows. He moved them aside to arrange himself more comfortably. Josie flicked open one of the afghans and covered herself.

"Cold?" he asked, feeling perfectly warm.

"No, but sometimes I like the weight of it. It's my emotional support afghan."

He coughed, trying to cover how cute he found that, found *her* in this moment. She must have been distracted by worry because she didn't feed him a lozenge. He missed them but was astute enough to realize how selfish that was and made himself focus on her instead.

She rested her head on the back of the couch, waiting for him to begin. He took her hand and held it in a friendly clasp.

"Let me begin by saying I haven't found anything pertaining to the threat against you. I've tried to pursue everything I've found that might be a viable lead, and nothing has led me to anyone who would want to threaten you. I kept an open mind, but I'm more convinced than ever that it was a random event, not specifically targeted to you."

Her lashes fluttered. "But that's good news, right? I'm safe."

"You're safe," he told her earnestly, giving her hand a squeeze.

"Why do I sense a but?" she said. Her voice quavered, and she cleared it.

"What do you know about your parents' relationship?"

She jumped, startled, cheeks flushing with dread, perhaps? "When I was little, they fought a lot. The house felt stressful. But it was a blip. Eventually they made up. By the time I was in middle school they seemed happy and everything was peaceful. Why?"

He took a breath, hating to shatter her illusions, her reality, her very foundation. "Josie, in the course of my investigation, I found something, something I think you need to know." He took another breath, a short one because the suspense was killing her. Her grip on his hand was painful now but he didn't shirk away. "Your dad had an affair with someone he worked with."

"No," she said, the word a breath.

"It lasted…a while."

"H-how long?"

"Two years."

Tears puddled in her eyes but didn't spill over. Her mouth was open but no sound came out. Tristan hurried on, letting his words fill the silence. "He and your mom separated for a few months. She gave him an ultimatum. He chose your family, ended the affair, and got a new job that didn't require travel. It seems like your parents' reconciliation was complete and, as you said, they've been doing their best to be happy and at peace since then."

She looked away from him, facing forward, and retrieved her

hand, tucking it over her waist as if trying to hold herself together. "My dad had an affair? My parents separated?"

He nodded.

"Why didn't I know about it?"

"You were young when it happened. No one wanted to tell you, to spoil your innocence."

The tears began to leak then, and she dashed at them. "So they let me go on in ignorance, let me believe a lie for two decades?"

"They were trying to protect you."

She whirled on him, angry. "Don't defend them."

"I'm not. I think it was wrong to keep you in the dark this long, that's why I told you."

She dashed her eyes again, nodding. "You're right. I know, I'm sorry. Kneejerk reaction and you got in the way of it."

"Hey, don't apologize. You're allowed to feel any way you want to feel right now. This is a big deal."

"Thank you," Josie said. She tipped forward, pressing her forehead to her knees. Her arms were still over her waist, trying to keep it together, trying not to fall apart. Tristan thought of what he knew of her family dynamic, of how hard everyone tried to keep Josie tamped down, under wraps, and contained, never wanting her feelings to get the better of her or be too big, and suddenly he couldn't take it anymore. Reaching over, he picked her up, set her in his lap and held her close.

"Let it out," he commanded. "Just let it go. It's all right."

She clutched his shirt and the dam broke, a drenching downpour of tears. Tristan didn't say a word, just held her and occasionally stroked her back or hair. Eventually, sooner than he would have expected, the tears came to an end.

"So that's what that feels like," she mused, sounding sleepy.

"What?"

"Having someone who is strong and secure enough to handle your emotional breakdown. Every time I cry, people tell me to stop. No one has ever told me to keep going before, and it's *so* nice. Thank you."

"It's okay, and you will be okay, Josie. You've got this."

"The irony is that I really think I do. I feel like this was the missing ingredient in being able to move forward, like I sensed this thing hanging over me. I assumed it was about me, that the threat and my subsequent reaction to it affected my parents so deeply they couldn't recover. But really their issues had nothing to do with me. I know it's selfish, but that's a huge relief. You can't imagine what it's like to believe you're the reason your family is on the verge of falling apart."

"I can imagine," he said.

She tipped her head back, studying him. "Do you want to talk about it?"

He shook his head.

"Because you don't want to talk about it, or because it's my turn to have an emotional breakdown and receive support?"

"Both."

"That's fair, as long as you know the offer is on the table. I'm here to listen and support without judgment."

Tristan didn't reply, and he didn't say what he was thinking, that she was only willing to offer support because she didn't know what it was. Everyone in his life had turned away from him because of the fallout of his actions. Why would Josie be any different?

CHAPTER 15

Josie at first had no idea what to do with the new information. For a few days she threw herself into her job and avoided her family. Her mind and heart were both whirring, but it wasn't necessarily a negative feeling. It shook her foundation to learn her father had an affair, to realize how close her family had come to falling apart. But the fact was that they *hadn't* fallen apart. It must have taken a tremendous amount of courage, forgiveness, and hard work for her parents to move past that time in their lives, to reclaim their relationship and seek reconciliation. To all outward appearances, they had. Tristan hadn't found any other evidence of another affair, and Josie's heart told her there hadn't been more. If they could reconcile and forgive each other, the least she could do was reconcile and forgive them, too.

Not quite ready to face her parents yet, she started with her siblings, asking them to meet for lunch on a Saturday a week after Tristan's bombshell revelation. As usual they seemed wary, but now Josie thought maybe this wariness had nothing to do with her. Before she blamed herself for their wariness. She was too big, too messy to fit into their well-ordered and perfect lives. But maybe their lives weren't as perfect as she'd always believed. Bart seemed to avoid intimacy, proved by the fact that he was thirty five and no closer to marriage than he had been when he was Josie's age. Janine's marriage was falling apart. Perhaps they weren't completely immune to the toll their parents' relationship took on their own. Maybe they *had* spared Josie by not telling her until she was ready to hear it, until she was an adult. Now she could face the complex issue with adult thoughts and feelings, instead of try to trod through it as an adolescent, like they had.

Bart was the first to arrive, which was unusual. Both her siblings were the type of people who believed early was on time and on time was late, but Janine seemed to take a special pleasure in being the first to show up for anything, much to Josie's annoyance. Josie preferred to be perfectly on time or even a few minutes later, giving her hosts a little extra to prepare. Mostly because, as a hostess, she knew how valuable those last few minutes could be. But what she viewed as a polite buffer, her sister had always viewed as slovenly tardiness.

"Hey," Bart said. He eased into the chair beside Josie and gave her a one-armed hug.

"Hey," she said, returning the hug full measure because that was a little sister's prerogative. He seemed to find that amusing, chuckling as he gave her a squeeze. "What's this about?"

"Let's wait for Janine," Josie suggested.

Bart frowned at the empty chair. "Since when do we have to wait for *Janine*?"

Josie sighed, trying to be magnanimous toward her often-annoying sister. "The divorce has thrown her into a tailspin. I'm going to be the bigger person and not even mention her lateness when she gets here." She made a show of zipping her lips, and Bart laughed again. Josie saw him through new eyes, too, thanks to Tristan. *I've rarely seen a brother adore his sister more.* Was that true? Did Bart adore her? Had he sacrificed himself on the family altar to save and protect her from the ugly truth of their parents' reality? If so, she owed him, even if it was a debt she'd never asked for.

Janine arrived then, looking huffy and unkept, a far cry from her usually perfect grooming. "What?" she snapped when she noticed Bart and Josie eyeing her.

"Everything okay?" Josie tried, careful to keep her tone neutral.

Janine gave a little nod, yanked out her chair, and sat down. "What's this about, Josie?"

"Can't I want to have lunch with my siblings?" Josie hedged.

"Yes, but when have you ever?" Bart returned.

"What? Of course I…" Josie began and trailed off. She had never called them merely to have lunch, she realized. In the rare times she'd suggested lunch in the past, it was usually to talk about holiday plans or what gift to get their parents for something. "Oh, well, maybe we should make it a thing. A once-a-month sibling luncheon to catch up on our lives."

"Sounds good," Bart said, smiling as he stared at his menu. The waitress came to take their order, and he spoke again. "So what is going on in your life? Catch us up."

"You're not engaged, are you?" Janine said, sounding horrified.

"What? No. Who would I be engaged to?" Josie said.

"Uh, the huge guy who has been following after you like a lost puppy lately," Bart said.

"You know he showed up at Mom's work," Janine said with the tattletale voice Josie loathed. "Her coworkers told her your new boyfriend was standing outside, mooning around, trying to decide if he wanted to talk to her about you."

"He's not my boyfriend, and he wasn't mooning. He had a legitimate reason to be there."

Bart was easing into big brother mode, the smile slipping into a grim set, eyebrow aloft. "What reason?"

Josie took a breath and let it out. "Tristan isn't my boyfriend. I used Grandpa's inheritance to hire him to look into the threat."

For a few beats there was a dreadful sort of silence, and then the bomb hit. "You did what?" Janine hissed.

"Josie, why? What a complete and utter waste," Bart said, touching his fingers to his temple as if in pain.

Josie held up her hands, waiting to speak until they got it all out.

"First of all it's my money to do with what I please. Second I think everyone has underestimated how much that event impacted my life because no one ever wanted to hear it. Everyone wanted me to let it go or *believed I made it up.*" She couldn't help but glance at Bart who had the decency to look sheepish. "But it's probably been one of the most impactful events in my life. I've been terrified all this time, always looking over my shoulder afraid..." she choked, cleared her throat, and pushed on. "Afraid to really live my life. I don't want to be afraid anymore. I wanted someone outside the situation, someone impartial, to take a look at the evidence and tell me what he thought."

"I wouldn't say he's impartial," Janine said in her usual caustic, sour tone.

"And what did he find?" Bart asked. His eyes darted between the two sisters, sifting, wondering how much Josie knew.

"He's finishing his final report, tying up some loose ends. But I'm fairly certain he's going to tell me it's nothing, that it was a one-off event by a loony guy intent on causing me emotional distress."

"And you're okay with that? With finally letting it go?" Bart said.

"Yes," Josie said, tone impassioned. "All I've *ever* wanted was to let it go, but I needed to be certain it was nothing. The rational part of me would convince myself it was, but then the fear would creep in and take over, would tell me it was real and he was out there, biding his time." Now she was the one to press her fingers to her temples. "It's been a nightmare."

"Why didn't you tell us?" Bart demanded.

"Because every time I tried, you told me to stop. You said I was blowing it out of proportion, being overly dramatic, being crazy. I know you agreed with Gabe that I was making it up."

Bart blanched. "I didn't, at least not completely. I hoped that was the case, but part of me knew better. It was easier to go along with one of your friends, who I thought was your boyfriend. It seemed like the best way to keep you safe."

"Gabe does not have my best interest at heart," Josie told him.

He rolled his eyes. "I know that *now.* Little weasel."

She laughed and rubbed a hand over her forehead, trying to keep a lid on her emotions, as well as the stress. She eyed Janine, who remained suspiciously silent, and took a breath. "In the course of his investigation, Tristan found some other stuff."

They tensed. Janine gripped the table. Bart cleared his throat. "What stuff?"

"About Mom and Dad. He told me about the affair, the separation. All of it."

"I told him not to," Bart groused, but he sounded an odd mix of aggrieved and relieved.

"I'm glad he did. That secret was too much for you, too much for both of you. Maybe I needed that protection when I was little, but I don't now. I'm an adult, and we're in this together, no matter what," Josie said and watched as Janine let out the breath she'd been holding and released her death grip on the table.

"How are you doing with everything?" Bart asked slowly.

Josie chose not to take offense that her family somehow always thought she was one breath away from a total breakdown. Instead she tried to take it as concern. "Okay," she said slowly. "I'm still processing, but so far, so good. And I haven't seen Mom and Dad yet, haven't talked to them about it."

"You don't have to," Janine blurted. A middle child, she liked to leave conflict buried. While Bart had likely been protecting Josie by keeping the secret all these years, Janine had been protecting herself. "They don't need to know you know."

"Yes, they do," Josie said definitively. "I'm tired of the secrets. They're toxic. If their relationship can weather Dad's affair, it can handle me knowing about it. We're going to get it all out in the open and move on and that will be that." She dusted her hands together. Bart smiled, looking perceptibly lighter. Janine bit her lip, still looking subdued and uncertain. Josie was certain enough for both of them, however. What their family needed, what they had needed the last two decades, was a little candid airing of dirty laundry. She would tell her parents the truth about Tristan, and they would talk about her dad's affair and the subsequent separation. And if Josie had her way, they would never keep secrets from each other again.

"I think you're wrong," Janine said, drawing Josie's attention back to her.

"About which part?" Josie asked, promising to keep a lid on her temper, no matter how her sister poked at her vulnerable spots.

"About Tristan. He wasn't some guy you hired. He likes you, I can tell. He couldn't keep his eyes off you that night we met him."

"Going to have to call an audible and agree with Janine on this one," Bart said, nodding his agreement. "The guy has Josie fever."

Josie's eyes fell to the table, cheeks flushed. "That's…he's…he's not my type," she said lamely.

Janine shrugged. "What does type matter? We know he likes you. I guess the only relevant question is how you feel about him." She leaned in, giving Josie a provoking big sister glance. "So tell us, Josie, how *do* you feel about him?"

"I…" Josie began, and then sagged in relief when she saw their waitress, loaded down with trays. "The food's here."

"Chicken," Bart accused, turning the word into a cough. Janine laughed, her first since she sat down, and the rest of the meal ended up being more fun than Josie could remember ever having with her siblings.

CHAPTER 16

A few days later Josie stood at the edge of Tristan's open office door and knocked. The knock was superfluous; he'd already noticed her. But it felt odd to see him in such an official looking place.

"Josie, hi. Come in."

"Hi, thanks."

"Sorry this is how you have to spend your day off school," he said.

"I don't mind. Different is always good."

He looked at her in that inexplicable way he had, as if she was something special and amazing instead of the same old Josie everyone else saw. It made her heart flip, that look. Tentatively, she entered the room and sat in the chair across from his desk. Tristan stared at her a moment longer in intense silence and then snapped to attention.

"So," he began.

"So," she returned, placing her hands in her lap to stop them from fluttering. "I brought my final check today, and I told Gaines he can feel free to use me for a referral or testimonial or whatever. I know I'm not your target audience, that you're hoping for bigger, richer fish, but hopefully my homespun earnestness will help anyone who is on the fence about hiring you." She was blabbering, and she needed to stop.

Tristan regarded her with his usual unsmiling intensity. "You're happy, then, with how we've handled you."

Her cheeks flushed, refusing to read anything more into the question than he probably intended. She nodded. "I know we maybe didn't see eye to eye in the beginning, but I really appreciate how you kept an open mind and delved deep to help me find closure."

"Even though I didn't actually find the guy?" he said.

"Yes. I always knew that was a longshot. What I really wanted, what I really *needed* was someone to listen and take me seriously, for someone to take an actual look into things and make certain it was okay. You did that better than I could have hoped for and..." she paused and took a breath, forcing herself to continue, to be *brave*. "You gave me a few gifts along the way, opening my eyes to some things in my life I needed to address. Gave me some good life wisdom."

"Wow, you make me sound amazing," he said.

"Well, it wasn't all good. You ate through two batches of lozenges. Speaking of, before I forget." She reached into her purse and presented him with two tins of her homemade cough drops. In true Josie fashion, she had customized the outsides of the tins, painting little mice on them in various scenes. Tristan picked them up and stared at them, one in each palm, heart exploding with too many things to process.

"Thank you," he said, voice raspy. "These are great. I don't want to eat them."

"If you eat them, I'll refill them," she offered with a nervous smile.

Their eyes met and lingered, and now Josie was the one who was overwhelmed. "You said you wanted to give me a final report."

He snapped to attention again and set the tins on his desk. "Yes. Sorry, okay, right." He rifled in his desk, looking for an actual report.

It was the closest Josie had come to seeing him flustered, and it was adorable. He finally located the report and set it on the desk. "Would you like me to itemize it or give you the big picture presentation?" He rested his hands on the report, fingers laced.

"Surprise me," Josie said, which made his cheek tick. He looked down and opened the report, his finger gliding along the page.

"So, I interviewed your friends and family, checked in with the officer in the original case, searched on the internet, tried to locate any cameras from that time, and set up a question with some dummy internet accounts. I did a security audit of your house and made recommendations. Additionally I would suggest that you take a basic self-defense course, carry some type of spray or weapon, mix up your routine, and develop strong situational awareness skills. But not because I think you're a target. I would suggest those things to anyone, especially women." He closed the report and rested his hands on it again. "Josie, I tried hard to keep an open mind, but I didn't find any evidence to suggest this was more than what it originally appeared to be, a lone psycho with an agenda to induce fear in a cute girl. I'm sorry, I wish I could give you more."

"Don't be sorry, Tristan. We've already established that you gave me exactly what I asked for, which is closure. This means a lot to me, so much. You have no idea. Last night I slept all night without waking."

"You did?" he said, eyes lighting.

"Yes," she declared with a cheerful head bob.

"I am so glad."

They stared at each other a few beats longer before Tristan remembered he was supposed to give her the report. "Here." He slid it across the desk.

"Thanks," Josie said. Their fingers brushed in passing and she paused, letting the touch linger. She stared at their joined hands, trying to re-up her floundering courage. "There's one more thing." Her eyes darted to his.

His brows rose, urging her to continue. "Yes?"

She took a breath and regretted it when it came out shaky. *Be brave, Josie.* She took another breath and blurted everything quickly, before she'd have to take another. "I know you didn't want to get personally involved when you were on my case, but since you're not anymore would you maybe want to go out sometime?" She pressed her lips together, willing the heat out of her cheeks. She had never, ever asked a guy out before. It was harder than she'd thought it would be, but it was also over in ten seconds. She could be brave in ten second bursts, apparently.

Tristan's jaw dropped, then closed, then opened again. Josie watched it work up and down with a dawning sense of horror until he finally said, "No."

She reached for the report between them, sliding it closer until it was in her grasp. "Oh, okay. No big deal." She picked up the report and stood.

"Josie," Tristan said, sounding miserable.

"It's fine. Don't worry about it. Thanks for this." She waved the report between them, wishing it could wave away all the awkwardness and make it dissolve. It turned out that rejection actually was worse than the fear of being rejected. Who knew?

"Josie," Tristan tried again, but he seemed to have no follow up beyond saying her name.

"I should go. Parking and..." she trailed off, wishing the floor would open up and provide an opening for her quick and painless death. Not that she would notice the pain at this point; it would have to be less than her psychic misery. "Anyway, take care."

"Josie," he tried one more time, but too late; she was already gone.

CHAPTER 17

S*ix Months Later*

"*I* love it here." Josie took a deep breath, one filled with fresh, clean air, and let it out slowly.

"It's pretty great," Eli agreed. They both leaned on the fence overlooking the goat pasture. At the moment their particular view was filled with mud and manure, but over all Eli's uncle's farm was fairly fantastic. Eli invited Josie a few months ago, and since then they'd been making treks to the country, sometimes with Gabe and sometimes without.

"How come you never invited me here before a few months ago?" she asked.

"I don't know. I guess I didn't realize how much you'd been going through since that thing in high school. You're pretty good at playing things close to your chest and hiding your emotions."

She laughed out loud, certain he was joking. A quick peek at his confused expression told her he wasn't. "Wait, seriously?"

"Yeah. You're so self-possessed and together, totally lacking in the crazy I've come to expect from the rest of your species."

"Wow, that's…you're the first person to ever say that to me. People tend to think I'm spastic," Josie said.

"I guess you are, compared to a robot. Compared to most regular people I know you've got yourself together. I mean, you have a job and a house and a car. Don't get drunk and make regrettable life choices, don't post insane, needy rants anywhere, and you've weathered Gabe the last decade. That alone should get you some kind of medal."

"Huh," she said, regarding him now instead of the goats. For the last few months, Eli had been edging closer, close enough to make Josie wonder if he was developing feelings for her, more than their usual friendship. He was her exact type: sweet, funny, and a little goofy. They'd been friends since high school and got along perfectly. More than got along, they had fun. She should be overjoyed at the thought. Instead she was wary and a little sad. Her traitorous heart thought briefly of Tristan and gave a ping.

Go away, she commanded her thoughts and feelings.

She had barely known him; hadn't dated him; was all wrong for him; had been epically rejected by him. Why, then, couldn't she seem to let him go?

"So," Eli drawled, staring hard at the goats. "I was thinking…"

"Yeesh, why can't they move this place closer to the city?" Gabe called, exiting his car.

"Oh, yay, Gabe's here," Eli said sarcastically, smiling when Josie snorted.

"Also, it smells," Gabe added.

"That's your upper lip," Josie returned.

"Har, har. I need to talk to you." Gabe flicked a glance to Eli.

"I'm sure anything you have to say to me can be said in front of Eli."

Eli, apparently heartened by this, eased what might have been protectively closer. Gabe scowled between them. "As it's nearly impossible to get you two apart these days, fine." He took a breath. "I have some bad news."

"You're quitting?" Josie guessed.

Gabe scowled. "What? No. Of course not."

"You got fired," she said.

He scowled harder. "Of *course* not. It's nothing to do with work. It has to do with us." He pointed between them.

Josie tossed a confused look to Eli, who shrugged. "What us?"

"You and me, Josie. I felt like I needed to give you a heads up that I'm seeing someone."

She blinked at him, still confused. "Okay. Congratulations?"

Gabe sighed, longsuffering. "I think it has the potential to be serious."

"I'm sure you'll find something to joke about eventually," Josie said and Eli snorted another laugh.

"Josie, come on. I don't want it to be weird between us," Gabe said.

"Wait," Josie drawled. "Are you...are you telling me this information because you think I'm going to be jealous or upset?"

"Aren't you?" Gabe said. "We work together. You're going to meet her eventually. I don't want it to be weird."

"I'm not certain anything with you ever could be not weird again," she said.

"Josie, we'll always be friends, okay, it's just...this happened. I wasn't expecting it."

She put her hands up. "Gabe, I'm going to try this one more time, so please listen. I am not in love with you. I have zero expectations of you or our life together. We're friends, barely even that anymore. I genuinely want you to be happy. If this girl makes you happy, go get her, tiger." She made a fist and thumped him on the bicep.

Gabe stared at her through narrowed eyes as if trying to comprehend her words. "Just please be nice to her when you meet her, okay? Don't make it weird. Mind if I use your uncle's toilet? It was a long drive." He turned and walked away before either of them could say anything.

"That was...so very Gabe," Eli said at last.

"What do you think it's like in his head?" Josie asked.

"I'm guessing there are a lot of mirrors, maybe some motivational posters that say, 'Get in there and find a way to make it about you,'" Eli said, smiling when she laughed. They turned back toward the goat pen. "Are you okay, though. For real?"

"Gabe is not my soul mate," she declared. "Despite what he believes. I feel like I should warn this girl, but I will not. I'm going to sit back and enjoy the slow moving train crash that will be their relationship." She cracked her knuckles.

"Not just that. I mean the other guy, Tristan. You've seemed a little…sad and withdrawn since you guys broke up."

"I thought you said I was good at keeping my emotions hidden."

"You used to be, but I've gotten to know you better." He smoothed his finger over the fence post in front of him. "We've been hanging out a lot lately."

"It's been nice," she said.

"Has it?" They faced each other. She could read what he was trying to say in his face, but she needed to hear the words, mostly because she had no idea what her answer would be. "Josie…"

He was interrupted by furious bleating. They turned to the pen again and saw one of the baby goats with its head stuck between two boards.

"Oh, man," Eli said. He began rolling up his sleeves, moving forward.

"Want some help," Josie asked.

"Nah, you'd better stay back. Its mom is territorial, don't want you to get butted on the first day of summer break."

She rested her elbows on the fence, smiling as Eli began wriggling the goat, attempting to free it while its mother stood anxiously nearby, shaking her head back and forth and pawing the ground.

"You'd better hurry or you're going to get a horn where the sun doesn't shine," Josie called.

"Which do you think feels worse, an appearance by Gabe or a horn up the butt?" Eli asked, grunting as he wriggled the boards.

Josie laughed and reached for her phone when it rang, not bothering to check the caller ID. "Hello," she said on a breathless laugh.

"Hi, Josie. This is Gaines Hillcrest."

"Oh, hi," she said, trying to orient her mind around the possible reason for his call. He probably wanted her to give a testimonial or referral, as she'd once promised.

"When is the last time you saw Tristan?"

"Um, six months ago, in his office. Why? Is he missing?" She gripped the phone tighter.

"No, I know where he is, but… Well, the fact is that he's in the hospital. And you're his emergency contact. They won't let me give permission to treat him. Could you possibly come here?"

⚷

Gaines couldn't tell Josie Tristan's condition, mostly because he didn't know. The hospital wouldn't tell him because he wasn't his emergency contact. *She* was. How? And why?

Those thoughts weren't foremost in her mind as she sped, literally, from the idyllic country farm to the vast hospital in DC, making record time on freeways that were usually littered with commuters. Hands shaking, she parked and ran to the hospital, pausing to catch her breath at the information desk. Gaines had told her which floor Tristan was on, but the wings of the hospital were color coordinated and Josie didn't know which way to go.

Once she was on the correct path—blue—she followed the line to the seventh floor and the surgery waiting room. Surgery? Why? What for?

A gunshot, as it turned out. Gaines stood when he saw her. "Here, she's here," he said, taking Josie by the arm and leading her to the desk. "She'll sign the form."

"What is the form? What happened? How is he?" Josie asked, hands shaking as she added her signature multiple times to she knew not what.

"You'll have to speak to the doctor," a bored looking receptionist told her. "He'll be with you as soon as I get these processed." She took the forms from Josie and closed the plastic divider between them, cutting off all contact.

"She closed the door," Josie said to Gaines, blinking in dismay.

"She's had a lot of practice doing it with me the last couple of hours," Gaines said. "Come back to the waiting room and sit down. I'll tell you what I know."

Josie followed him back to the waiting room where she noticed a petite blond woman who stood at Gaines's approach, wringing her hands in concern. "Any word?" she asked.

Gaines shook his head. "Jordan, this is Josie. Josie, my wife, Jordan."

"Hi," Josie said, offering Jordan a smile. Jordan gave her one in return, snagging Gaines's hand as they sat side by side. He chafed her hand in both his, but Josie thought it was a gesture to soothe himself instead of his wife. It must be nerve wracking when an employee was injured.

"What happened? What do you know?" Josie asked.

"All I know is that he was shot," Gaines said. When Josie's jaw dropped and her pupils dilated, he hastened to add, "I don't think it's critical. This isn't the ward for that, and they would have granted him emergency surgery without permission, if so."

"But he must have been unconscious, if he couldn't sign for himself," Josie reasoned.

"Yeah. Let's try not to panic until we hear the details," Gaines said. Jordan used her free hand to rub his back soothingly, and he tossed her a smile. Josie looked away, feeling like a peeper on their intimate little tableau.

After another helpless twenty minutes, a doctor appeared and called Josie's name. She stood, feeling wobbly with fear and anxiety. "Tristan was shot through the forearm. The bullet ricocheted, grazing and shattering a bone, but most of the damage was contained to the tendons and muscles. We're going to do some repair work with the surgery, but he'll be looking at some therapy for a few weeks to recover."

"Why is he unconscious?" Josie asked.

"He was on some kind of platform, when he fell. The force of the shot knocked him off and he struck his head, knocking him unconscious."

"Is he going to have damage from that?"

"It appears to be a contusion and hairline skull fracture. We're keeping an eye on him, but there's no brain swelling or bleeding. All in all, given how much worse everything could have gone, it's best-case scenario. We're prepping him now, we'll take him back as soon as the OR is ready. This is going to be a lengthy surgery, a few hours at least. You can check his progress on that television screen. When he's in recovery, someone will come for you."

"Okay, thank you," Josie said, nodding.

The doctor disappeared and she and Jordan and Gaines looked at each other. "You can go," Gaines said.

Now Jordan and Josie looked at each other. "Which one of us are you talking to?"

He smiled. "Both. Honey, go pick up the kids. Josie, go get sleep or supper or whatever. I'll stay and let you know how it turns out."

"No," Josie heard herself say. If she was his emergency contact, it must have been for a reason, or at least she decided to take it as one. "They might need more from me, more signatures or permission or… or something." She had no idea, only that now that she was here, she didn't want to go away again. "You two both go, I'll be fine here. I saw a nice gift store downstairs. I'll grab a coffee and a book and be fine. And I'll let you know when he's out of surgery, etcetera."

"I feel like I should stay," Gaines said.

Josie smiled. "I feel like you should go feed your wife and children. I'll let him know you were here and I had to fight you for it, he'll love that."

Gaines laughed. "He'll hate that."

"You're right, but I'll love telling him that," Josie amended.

"I can see I'm not going to win this one, and I'm not sure Tristan would want me to. I'd appreciate hearing any information you receive," Gaines said.

"It was really nice to meet you," Jordan said. "Maybe once all this is over we can all get together. I didn't even know Tristan had a girlfriend."

"He doesn't, but apparently he has whatever I am. In any case I would love to get together sometime, and it was really nice to meet you, too," Josie said, offering her a smile.

She waited until they were gone and then headed downstairs for coffee, a muffin, and a book, curling into one of the uncomfortable chairs to try and settle her mind enough to read. Thoughts kept trying to intrude, and she kept batting them away, knowing she wouldn't receive any answers until Tristan woke up.

"Mr. Evans is awake, if you'd like to see him now."

Impossibly, Josie had fallen asleep. She woke to the hushed and mellow voice of the attendant, alerting her to Tristan's progress. "Yes," Josie blurted. She reached for her purse, intending to do a repair on her face, before realizing the woman was waiting to take her along. She stood and swept a finger under each eye and pinched her cheeks, working her mouth up and down to try and erase the hospital dryness of artificial and recirculated air.

The woman led her to a large room, filled with bays of unconscious or semi-conscious people, separated by curtains. Josie followed her to the last curtain in the row.

"There you go," the woman said.

"Thank you," Josie replied in an equally hushed whisper. Hands shaking again, she reached for the curtain and pulled it back, wincing when it made a harsh mechanical screeching sound of metal on metal. Tristan slept on, thoroughly unaware of the noise or Josie or anything else. He was bandaged, his free hand hooked to an IV and pulse-ox monitor. Otherwise he looked exactly like the man she left six months ago, the one she declared her feelings for and who soundly rebuffed her. Her cheeks flushed with remembered embarrassment. Even so she edged closer, leaning over the bed to drink in the sight of him. Usually people looked smaller and more fragile in those flimsy hospital gowns, but not Tristan. He looked buffer and more ripped, as if he'd thrown himself into his workouts with extra vigor.

Josie stood at the edge of his bed, hands clasped nervously around her purse, wishing he would wake up, wishing he would sleep until she was gone. Now that she'd seen him, it was probably safe to go away. On the other hand she should definitely check in, make certain he didn't need anything else. Did he have a cat? A dog? A *wife*? She'd never asked, and he'd certainly never volunteered.

She pulled out her phone to text Gaines when she heard a whispered rasp.

"You cut your hair."

She glanced up to see him eyeing her with his usual toe-curling intensity. "You cut a hole in your arm."

He blinked sleepily a couple of times and then he did the impossible: he laughed. Josie stared at him mesmerized, unused to the sound, and then edged forward farther and perched on his bed. His free hand sought her, resting on her bare knee. "I missed you so much."

"Yeah?" she said.

"Every minute of every day," he rasped. His thumb slid along the inside of her knee, making her shudder.

"Are you married?" she asked.

"No, never," he said, wincing.

"Then why…" it was probably bad etiquette to ply a man for answers when he was a half hour off anesthesia, but Josie was more than a little confused by him. In retrospect maybe now was the best time because he seemed more open than usual. Apparently the key to getting him to let her in was to shoot him, knock him unconscious, then give him high levels of painkillers and general anesthesia.

"Because reasons…lots of reasons," Tristan muttered, eyes going closed. They flapped open when Josie pressed forward and kissed him. "Why'd you do that?" he asked.

"Because reasons, lots of reasons," she said, stroking a finger on his cheek.

"You taste even better than the pep'mint mocha," he slurred, eyes going closed again.

"So do you," she said, stealing one more kiss before she lost him to sleep.

She texted Gaines and sat vigil until Tristan was moved to his permanent room for the night. He stirred when they transferred him from the portable bed to the one in his room, eyes on Josie with that signature flaming intensity. She fussed while the nurses did their thing, pouring him a cup of water, acquainting herself with the remote. When they were finally alone she held the cup of water for him as he drank through the straw, eyes still on her. She set the water aside and faced him.

"Will it hurt if I sit with you?" she asked.

"It might hurt if you don't," he said.

She eased in beside him and fussed with the covers, making certain he would be warm and cozy.

"You're my little nurturer," he said.

She froze and regarded him. "I didn't know I was your anything."

"In my mind, you're my everything." He rested his head on the bed, too sleepy to hold it up any longer.

"Why only in your mind?" she asked, mimicking his pose. They stared at each other nose to nose.

"Because...reasons."

"You must write poetry," she said, pressing her palm to his cheek, fingers rasping over his beard stubble.

He closed his eyes, leaning in to her touch. "Josie," he said, the word cut short when she kissed him. "Are you ever going to let me kiss you first?"

"You've had a six month window of opportunity," she said.

"But I was unconscious for this last part."

"You're not unconscious now," she said, heart thumping.

"Keep an eye on my monitor, I might stroke out," he said. Easing forward, he kissed her, and it was better, so much better than anything that came before.

"Exactly what I thought," he said when the kiss was over.

"What is?"

"You're addictive," he said and fell asleep again.

Josie stayed. There was no reason for it. She had assured herself he was okay, but still she didn't leave.

"Are you missing work?" he asked, the next time he woke. It was three AM after a nurse checked his vitals, but he was becoming more lucid as the anesthesia left him.

"Summer break," she said. She had moved to the chair when she decided to stay, not wanting to disturb his slumber or assume too much. "Let's play a game."

"Ping pong?" he suggested.

"You'd still beat me. I stink at sports that involve a ball," she said. "But I bet you don't."

He didn't reply.

"Admit it, you played football."

After an internal debate he said, "I did."

"I bet you were really good."

"No, I was kind of mediocre," he said. She eyed his impressive physique with disbelief. "Maybe if I went to a different school I would have been better or at least stood out more."

"What was wrong with your school?" she asked, anxious for more insight he might give her into him and his life. Or any, really.

"Nothing, but it was massive. We had a big talent pool, and only the best guys played ball."

"Did you get a scholarship to play in college?"

"No, but that's less about ability than other things."

"What other things?" she asked sincerely. She loved to learn new things, and this was definitely brand new information.

"It's not like on TV where a recruiter shows up and notices a kid who plays well. Kids need someone to advocate for them, their families and coaches."

"And you didn't have that," she guessed.

He shook his head. "What's your game?"

"This is the game. I ask as many questions as I want and try to get you to answer."

"Where's the fun in that?" he asked.

"The fun is in seeing how far I can push you," she said.

"Where's the fun for me?" he amended.

"This is my game. You'll have to come up with your own."

His eyes brightened and fell to her lips, but he said nothing.

"Have you always lived in DC?" she asked.

He paused, then, "No. I moved here two weeks before we met. Hence I put you as my emergency contact, because you were the only person besides Gaines I knew."

"Is that the only reason?"

He shook his head.

She waited him out.

"Wishful thinking on my part," he admitted, reaching for her hand and clasping it gently in his. His thumb smoothed over her fingers.

"Where did you come from?"

"Existentially?"

"Literally."

Another pause, then, "Do you promise you won't Google me?"

"You're assuming I haven't."

His eyes widened with something like fear. She gave his hand a reassuring squeeze. "I haven't, I won't. I'd rather hear it from you."

"Missouri."

"Show me."

"As if we've never heard that before," he said, but he was almost smiling.

"Why did you leave your home?"

He remained silent and stoic.

"Why did you come here?" she tried.

"For the job. I saw Gaines's listing, interviewed, got the job, and moved away within a three day time span."

She wondered if he had been running toward a new life or away from the last one. "Did you go to college?"

"I have a two year associates degree," he said.

"In what?" she asked.

"Criminal justice."

"Were you a cop?"

Another pause, this one longer. "Yes."

"Why did you answer that one?" she said.

"Because given my degree and my personality, it was probably easy to figure out the answer for yourself," he said.

"You have definite cop vibes. Also the haircut."

"You don't like my hair?" he asked.

"How does saying you have cop hair mean I don't like it?" she returned.

"So you do like my hair?" he asked, an odd mix of groggy and flirtatious.

"What's not to like?" she asked, reaching out to streak her fingers through his crop top. He closed his eyes and sighed the way her parents' dog did when she scratched his sweet spot. She didn't ask him what she most wanted to ask him, *Why did you turn me down when I asked you out?* But this meeting had been a confirmation of what she originally suspected—he had feelings for her. How deep they ran, she had no idea. But they were there, she hadn't imagined them.

"Josie," he said, sounding suddenly sleepy.

"What?"

"Come lay beside me again," he said softly, more than a hint of vulnerability in his tone. Josie complied, crawling beside him and nestling close. To her surprise, Tristan nestled, too, resting his head on her shoulder as he took a deep breath.

"You're always sniffing me," she said, half accusing, half questioning.

"Yes," he agreed. His eyes were closed, but he found her shoulder and kissed it.

"Why?" she demanded, when it became apparent he wouldn't answer.

"Because you smell better than anything I've ever smelled before." He paused, eyes still closed, then opened his eyes, swallowed hard, and added, "Josie, you smell like home."

Home now or home before? She wondered but wasn't certain how to ask. Did she remind him of something from his past? "What does home smell like?" she asked instead.

"Sweet and soft and warm and wonderful."

She grimaced. "Those are Grandma smells."

He opened one eye and squinted at her, amused. "No, baby, no."

Now it was her turn to let out a breath, frustrated at the answers she couldn't find, the ones he refused to provide. At the same time she felt the almost desperate need to soak up whatever bit of softness he was now willing to give, certain it would disappear when he returned completely to himself.

Josie slid her arms around his middle, careful not to jostle him or touch his injured arm. "Tristan," she whispered.

"Hmm," he murmured, halfway between sleep and awake.

"Don't push me away again when you wake up," she pled.

"I'll…try," he said slowly, carefully.

"We should have a safe word, in case you start doing it, I can tell you to stop."

"Maybe," he murmured, eyes too heavy to open.

"Maybe's a weird safe word," Josie murmured sleepily in reply, smilng when he chuckled. A moment later, they were both asleep.

CHAPTER 19

The next time they woke, weak light filtered through the edge of the hospital window. Tristan woke first so when Josie finally opened her eyes, they saw him looking at her. She couldn't read the expression on his face, but it wasn't good.

"We didn't find a safe word," she lamented.

"Josie," he said tightly.

"Don't do the thing," she whispered.

"Josie," he said, the words wrenched out with a grimace.

"It doesn't have to be anything more than it is right now," Josie added.

His hand clamped on her wrist. Her hasty flow of words ran out, but she looked at him with big, baleful eyes. He took a shallow breath and forced the words through dry lips. "Can you call the nurse and ask for some pain reliever?"

Josie jumped as if she'd received a shock. "Oh. Goodness, you poor guy. I guess all your anesthesia finally ran out. Hold on." The call button was on the other side of him. In order to reach it and avoid jostling his injured arm, Josie sat high up on her knees and leaned far over, inadvertently pressing her stomach onto his face.

Far from being disturbed, or even smothered, Tristan relaxed and inhaled, making a little sound that, if Josie didn't know better, sounded a lot like contentment.

After she called the nurse she stood, rooted in her purse, and handed him a little stick. He didn't take it, mostly because he had no idea what it was.

"What is that?"

"Honey," she said.

He blinked.

She pinched the top of the tube, popping it open. "It's a honey stick Eli gave me. Honey is a natural pain reliever."

"What am I supposed to put it on?" he asked, smiling when she tittered.

"You don't smear it on anything; you eat it." She tipped it closer, watching as he sucked down the little bit of honey. When she was satisfied that he'd eaten it all, she gave him some water, adjusted his blanket, then retrieved a washcloth, wrung it out, and placed it on his forehead. All the while Tristan watched her, gaze intent and unblinking.

When she returned with the re-wet washcloth and eased closer to place it on his forehead, he caught her wrist.

"Eli gave you honey?"

"Yes, although when you say it, it sounds loaded with more meaning. His uncle keeps bees and makes honey products."

His Adam's apple bobbed. "Are you two together?"

"No," she whispered.

He swallowed again, convulsively this time, and relaxed enough to drop her wrist. She almost hated to continue, but for the sake of honesty she needed to, so she perched on the edge of the bed, twisting the hem of the cheap sheet.

"We've been spending a lot of time together. Nothing has happened, but lately it's been feeling like it might, if we let it."

"Is that what you want?" he asked, voice tight.

Josie was quiet for a long time, thinking, trying to sort through her confusion. "I feel like it's what I should want." She chanced a glance at him and saw that his expression was keen, but not angry or upset. "Eli has been a good friend, he's a good guy, and he's my usual type." She peeked at him again and noted the grim set of his features. "Maybe this is a discussion for after your pain reliever kicks in."

"Can't imagine it will hurt less then," Tristan said.

She leaned forward and stroked his forehead. "Who shot you?"

"I don't know," he said.

"You can't remember?"

"I never saw him, walked into a trap." He took her hand, thumb smoothing over her fingers. "Josie…"

Josie felt immediate dread, certain he was going to try and push her away. "Is the honey helping?" she blurted. "You seem a little less distressed than a few minutes ago."

"It's not the honey; it's the Josie," he said, bringing her fingers to his lips.

"You're so suave." Her mind filled in the blanks of all the other women he must have practiced on.

"I'm really not," he said. If he were suave, he'd figure out a way to tell her everything, instead of stare at her with heart emoji eyes like a lovesick teenager. "The thing you need to know is…"

The nurse's arrival interrupted him. She had to check his wristband against her computer before she could dole his medication, then she asked him a series of questions and checked his vitals. When she was finally finished, the doctor arrived, asked the same questions, checked the chart, and made an inspection of Tristan's wound.

"How would you like to go home today?" the doctor asked, his bright, upbeat tone a sharp contrast to Tristan's flat affect.

"I would like it very much," Tristan said evenly. Despite the lack of inflection, Josie knew how much he meant it.

"Great. Obviously you won't be able to drive and do other mundane tasks for a while. Your wife here will have to play chauffer a while." He tossed Josie a smile, which she returned. Tristan shifted uncomfortably, about to interject, but Josie grabbed his good hand and gave it a squeeze.

"Absolutely. This is the only way he'll let me drive," she said.

Tristan groaned, either at the prospect of her driving or at inconveniencing her, she had no idea. They watched the doctor make a few notes, and then he was gone, and they were alone.

"Josie," Tristan began, but again Josie cut him off.

"I know what you're going to say."

"I bet you don't," he said.

She continued undaunted. "You're going to say you're macho and manly and will find a way to drive yourself and do all the things, but you don't have to when I'm available and I'm here. School is out, I am at your beck and call for the next few weeks. As a, you know, as a *friend*. I would do the same for anyone." She fidgeted with the hem of her shirt now. If he had wondered what her wardrobe would be once it was too warm for sweaters, he wondered no longer. Today she wore a t-shirt with pugs all over it, hundreds of them now staring at him with bulgy eyes and lopsided tongues.

"Josie," he began.

"You need someone, Tristan," she said, tone impassioned.

With his good hand, he yanked her close and kissed her. When the kiss was over, she sat back a little stunned. "Good to know that works," he said, sitting back against the bed. The problem was that it worked on him, too, so he forgot what he originally wanted to say. Josie stared at him with big eyes and messy hair and he wanted to pull her close again, to kiss her and hold her and never let her go. The prospect of spending a few weeks with her this summer was almost too good to be true, almost more than he could bear, and that brought him back full circle.

"The thing is, the guy who shot me..."

She wriggled and sat up, suddenly alert. "You know who shot you?"

He shook his head. "No, but I think I know why. The reason I went there in the first place was because I got a lead on the whisper network."

She squinted. "What's a whisper network?"

"Rumor mill. I put out some questions on a few websites. One of them hit and I went to track the lead."

"Okay," she said softly.

He reached for her hand again. "The lead was about an old case I thought I'd wrapped up."

Josie's heart started to thrum with dread and anticipation, because somehow she knew. "It was about me, wasn't it?"

He nodded. "Someone said he knew the man who threatened you. I went to learn more, not realizing it was an ambush."

"And you were *shot*," she said, feeling miserable, and then resolved. She sat a little straighter and put her shoulders back. "That settles it then, you're mine for the summer. Because now I owe you."

CHAPTER 20

"I said owe," Josie reiterated after Tristan was safely buckled in the car. He had thought she'd said "own" earlier, and it amused him. So much that he almost laughed, if a cheek twitch counted as a laugh. With Tristan, it definitely did.

"You own me?" he'd said, eyebrows aloft, amusement ratcheting higher when Josie's cheeks flushed crimson. But the nurse had entered then to start Tristan's discharge, so she'd only had time to hiss a soft, "*No,*" before they were interrupted.

Tristan watched her as she adjusted the automatic seat forward. "Settle in, now's your chance to obtain a doctorate in the time it takes me to reach the steering wheel," she said, and it did seem to take an inordinate length of time to for the seat to stop moving, her feet sticking out straight, straining for the pedals.

Tristan watched her, feeling a thousand different things. He had no idea how he'd made it this long without her. Worse, he had no idea how to ever undo it and go back to the way it was.

"You do not owe me," he tried.

She finally reached the front of the car and buckled herself in. "You were shot in service to me. In some countries I'm not released from that debt until I'm shot in service to you."

"What countries?" he asked.

She squinted. "I was not prepared for follow up questions to that statement. Countries of old," she flung out. "The Wild West. Codes of valor. Etcetera."

"Are you throwing out random masculine words and phrases in the hope that I'll let this go?" Tristan asked.

"Chivalry," she continued undaunted. "Rules of warfare. Etcetera." She paused to reverse out of the parking space, continuing to speak after she was on the roadway. "The point is that I do, indeed, owe you."

"Indeed you do not," he returned.

"Don't say indeed," she chastised.

"You just said indeed," he pointed out.

"I'm the kind of quirky geek who can say indeed and have it be normal. On you it's..." she bit her lip.

"Forced?" he guessed.

"Hot," she blurted, then bit her lip harder, trying to reel the words back in.

"I forgot you like nerds," he said, sounding dismal.

"You don't like girls like me," she said.

"You don't know what I like," he said. His tone was customarily flat, but the words still did something to her, something that made her swallow and grip the wheel.

"Where are we going here?" she asked. Ribs was sending them to a safe house for a couple of days to make certain no one was hot on their trail. He had arrived at the hospital with a hand-drawn map, which was Josie's first inkling that there were people in the world who didn't trust computers or phones to transmit information. *Unless you know for certain something isn't being hacked, assume it is,* Tristan had told her after Ribs left.

"Keep going north," Tristan said.

"It's cute how you think I know which direction I'm going," Josie replied. "I'm on road, that's as much directional information as my brain allows me."

"Keep going on road until I say otherwise," Tristan replied. He wasn't looking at a map, was relatively new to the area she'd lived in all her life, and still apparently knew how to navigate better. And so bad was she with directions that she didn't question him on it.

They drove in silence a while. Josie worried Tristan might have fallen asleep and she would get lost, but eventually he reached over and rested his hand on her thigh, a surprisingly intimate touch that made her synapses spring to life and begin firing warning shots at each other.

"Is this okay?" he asked, noting that she squirmed a couple of times.

"It's like in those movies when someone walks into a power plant that hasn't been used in decades and trips the power and all these weird looking machines whirr to life and then a message pops up on a giant screen behind the hero," Josie said.

Tristan blinked at her.

She cleared her throat. "Or something. Hey, is that a dead mink?"

"Groundhog," Tristan said without taking his eyes off her. "What does the message say?"

"What?" she asked.

"The message, on the screen behind the hero. What does it say after such long disuse?"

Josie's cheeks flushed, with pleasure this time. Not only had he understood her convoluted simile about the way his touch made her feel, he wanted to know more about it. "It's probably a warning."

"About what?" Tristan prodded, his thumb smoothing along the outer edge of her leg, making her incoherent. Not that she needed much help.

"Not to repeat past mistakes."

"What past mistakes?" he asked.

Josie thought about that before she answered, thought about every guy she'd been with and all the different ways they'd wounded her. Most of those wounds had been slight, misunderstandings and missed signals that led to a mutual parting of ways. There had only ever been one thing that hurt her, that cut her to her core in a way that had the power to shape her life, was still shaping her life.

"It would say, 'Don't repeat the mistake of believing you mean as much to someone as they mean to you.'"

Tristan studied her as Josie studiously drove. "I'm not Gabe."

She reached a stoplight and faced him. "The problem is not that I think you're Gabe; the problem is that I don't know who you are, and without knowing that I don't know in which particular way you might hurt me."

Instead of reassuring her, he broke eye contact and faced forward. "That's true. The light changed. Merge onto that ramp up there."

She did as he indicated, increasing her speed to match traffic after the merge. "What do you think a safe house is like?" she asked when traffic slowed enough for her to talk.

"Dingy, if I had to guess."

"You've never used one?" she asked.

"I was a cop. Not a lot of call for safehouses," he said.

"Yes, but you're so cool like that."

"Cool like what?"

"Secret agent stuff. It all seems within your wheelhouse, more your wheelhouse than mine."

"I'm not certain cop is closer to safehouse than kindergarten teacher; I think we're equidistant," he mused.

"Well, then we have this thing in common."

She seemed inordinately pleased by that, smiling vaguely to herself even as someone cut her off. Tristan gripped the seat with his good hand, certain they were about to slam into the back of the guy.

"You're a nervous passenger," Josie noted, slowing her pace as the person in front of them sped up, only to be replaced by someone else who honked as he darted in front of them.

"Can't imagine why," Tristan said, dabbing a bead of sweat on his upper lip.

"Everyone's always in such a hurry all the time," Josie noted as another car swerved around them.

"Maybe you should go a little faster," Tristan suggested.

"I'm already going the speed limit," Josie returned. "They're the ones who are speeding. They're wrong. *You're wrong.*" She leaned forward to yell the last part as another car whipped around them.

"Sometimes you have to do what's wrong to stay alive," Tristan noted, heart picking up its pace as the possibility of their demise grew stronger with each car that passed them.

"I don't follow what the crowd does," Josie told him, placidly gripping the wheel.

"Even if you die?" Tristan asked.

"Even if I die," Josie replied.

"Even if *I* die?" he tried.

She darted him a glance, sighed softly, and increased her speed by ten miles an hour. By the time she exited the highway she was frowning. "I feel like I lost something," she noted.

"I feel like I'm about to," he agreed, pressing a hand to his stomach. "Maybe I should drive."

"You can't drive," she argued.

"Josie, neither can you," he said. He had counted no less than seven people who flipped them off as they whipped around their car.

"I don't take the interstate much," she admitted. She darted him a glance and saw him staring raptly into space. "Are you actually sick? Do you need a soda?"

He shook his head, trying to focus hard on his thoughts. One of them was trying to escape, and he needed to pin it down before it got away. He had discounted two possibilities when it came to Josie. The first was that she was an innocent victim and somebody targeted her by chance. The second was that she had done something bad to deserve being targeted. Now a third, more ephemeral possibility presented itself: what if Josie had made herself a target by doing something *good*? What if she had been so intractable in some way that she had become an obstacle to be dealt with? She'd said it herself: she positively would not budge. What if someone needed her to budge, enough to threaten her? What if her refusal to budge had made someone so angry they wanted to kill her then? Wanted to kill her now?

Tristan reached out a hand and rested it on her leg again, soothing her preemptively with his touch. "We need to go over everything again. Everything from your past. We're missing something. Turn left on that road."

"I don't even see a road," she muttered.

"That's kind of the point of a safehouse, I think."

"This seems fishy to me," she said.

"Ribs is trustworthy; he wouldn't give us a bogus safehouse."

"No, I meant that literally. This is fishy. Something stinks like dead fish."

The car meandered a few more times, and they discovered the source of the smell, a houseboat on the river.

"A houseboat," Josie exclaimed in surprise. "That's fancy."

Tristan didn't want to trample her excitement, so he kept his thoughts to himself, but what he thought was that he hoped the place was actually better than it looked. And smelled.

CHAPTER 21

"This is, um…" Josie's words trailed away along with her excitement as they headed inside.

"It's very um," Tristan agreed, scanning the small space. Suddenly he knew how his boss was able to score the place so fast, with almost no notice. "I bet Ribs owns this place." It had all the earmarks of the kind of project a former navy guy would sink his teeth into. He had likely bought it for cash, intending to fix it up. A couple of projects in the kitchen had already been started, adding credence to the theory.

"That makes me feel better, actually. For a minute I was getting crack den vibes."

"That actually is my wheelhouse, and there are no drugs here."

"How can you tell?" she asked.

"The smell."

She faced him, hands on hips and a speculative smile on her face. "You're like a tracker hound. What else can you smell?"

He eased closer and leaned in, until his nose was near her neck but not touching. "Pumpkin. Vanilla."

"That's not me, then. I switch scents with the season."

He sniffed harder, touching his nose to her skin. "Grapefruit and bergamot."

"Incredible," she whispered, threading her fingers through his hair.

"Yes, it is," he agreed, lips now skimming her neck.

"Doesn't it hurt your wound to bend like that?" she whispered.

"Immensely," he said, groaning as he stood straight.

With a little chuckle, she led him to a padded bench and pressed him to sit, rubbing a comforting little circle on his good shoulder. "What can I get you? Would you like a drink of water?"

"I don't know," he said.

"You don't know if you're thirsty?" she clarified.

"I don't know how to respond to people fussing over me, taking care of me," he responded truthfully.

Josie kept up the comforting little routine on his shoulder, but leaned in to kiss his cheek, pausing to whisper, "Then let's teach you."

His eyes tracked her as she moved around the tiny kitchen, checking cupboards. "Hey, it's stocked with food."

"How else would we eat?" Tristan mused. It wasn't as if they could easily leave, now that they were here, not until they'd been cleared by Ribs.

Josie opened the fridge and leaned in, exclaiming again, "This is real food, like home-cooked Mom stuff."

"Jordan probably. She always sends stuff with Gaines that smells edible," Tristan said.

She closed the refrigerator door and leaned against it. "If we're living on their boat and eating their food, does that mean we're now Gaines and Jordan?"

He shook his head. "Something is missing."

"What?" she asked.

"Jordan's five months pregnant." He wagged his brows, eyes falling to her midsection.

"That escalated quickly," she said.

"Look at those pink cheeks," Tristan noted.

Josie studiously ignored him. "Do you think the water works on this boat?"

"I hear a hum of some sort, so probably." He had no idea if they were on a generator or engine, and he was too tired to investigate, trusting the boat's function to Ribs's earlier visit.

"Here's what we're going to do: I'm going to shower, and you're going to nap."

He wrinkled his nose. "I haven't napped since…I don't know if I've ever napped."

"I know, you're very macho," she soothed, going forward to help him off the bench and into the tiny cabin with the little bed.

"How come you get to shower and I don't?" he complained, although he allowed her to lead him without any fuss.

"Next time I get a hole punched through my body, it can be my turn to nap while you take the shower," she promised as she tucked him into bed and arranged the covers around him.

He watched her fuss, subdued and silent, then took her hand, anchoring her in place before she could escape. "'Next time' makes it sound like you have more togetherness planned for us."

She hovered over him, trying and failing to read his face. "I can't plan what you won't allow."

"Josie," he began, tone somber and regretful.

She interrupted whatever he was about to say, brushing her lips softly on his. "Get some sleep, Tristan."

He didn't think he would sleep. He liked to be the one on watch, after all, and it went against every instinct to believe he was weak and helpless. But when he next opened his eyes the room was dark. His ears strained, listening for sounds of Josie, for sounds of anything except the quiet lapping of the water outside.

Why was it so silent? Had something happened to Josie? Before he could investigate, Josie stepped into the doorway, backlit by light from the main portion of the cabin.

"Hey," he said, voice croaky. "How did you know I was awake?"

"I heard you rustling alertly."

She couldn't see him, so he allowed himself a smile. "What does rustling alertly sound like?"

"Like a beefy cop who wakes up afraid and doesn't like it," she said, taking a step inside.

"That's an apt description," he agreed. "I didn't like the silence."

"I was reading."

"What were you reading?" he asked. Had Jordan stocked the boat with books?

"Purse book. What were you going to use to come to my defense, if I was in trouble?" she asked curiously, perching on the edge of the bed.

He opened the nightstand and pulled out the gun Ribs had told him about, holding it aloft for her inspection.

"Of course you're the type of guy who would always have a gun handy, even on a boat," she said.

"Of course you're the type of woman who would have a book handy, even on a boat," he returned. "At least mine can defend you in an emergency."

"You haven't seen the size of my book," she said, and it was everything he could do to stop himself from laughing.

"What have you got going on here?" he asked, tugging at her odd assortment of clothes.

"I cobbled some stuff together from what I could find. Also, either your employer or his wife bought us each a pack of underpants. Not sure how to feel about that. Bad news, though."

He tensed, preparing himself for the worst. "What?"

"No makeup." She pointed to her face.

"You wear makeup?" he said.

"See, when said with no inflection, it's really hard to tell if that's an attempt to make fun of me or compliment me," she said.

He took her hand and kissed her fingers. "It can be both. To be clear, you look the same to me either way."

"That's not actually clear," she said, frowning slightly.

"It's not?" he returned, giving her hand a solid tug so she was forced to lie down beside him, stretching her body the length of his good side as his arm slid around her, cinching her against him.

"Maybe you like keeping ugly things close by, as some sort of ascetic punishment. Like 'pain is pleasure, torture is benefit.'"

He cleared his throat. "I'm going to need a lozenge soon." His hand slipped beneath her hair, thumb sliding along her neck.

"Okay, but I only have a few left in my purse."

"We'll have to wrap this up quickly, then. We can't be without those."

"I tried some new recipes," she admitted. "Based on the ones you gave me." Because she missed him, because she'd wanted the reminder of him, even when it was painful, even when it was a blatant memento of his rejection.

"What did you think?"

"It was interesting, but the original was better. I guess I'm boring that way."

"I'm not certain anyone who makes her own lozenges could ever be considered boring," he said.

Josie frowned into the darkness above them. He sounded so... approving and besotted. But how could that be? He had rejected her, boldly and painfully. She had blurted her feelings for him, given him ample opportunity to reciprocate, and he hadn't. And then he hadn't called her, in all their time apart. Surely that was because he didn't want to be with her, didn't find her attractive. Was it because of things like the lozenges? Of course it was, it had to be. She wasn't and had never been anyone's idea of normal, nor had she wanted to be. Josie had worked hard her entire life to be original, to march to the beat of her own drum. She had dated men who were looking for the sort of person she was. Tristan, conventional and pragmatic, must find her as humiliating and cringey as her straitlaced family did. And that thought was so painful it had the power to devastate her. She had stayed safe in her little bubble, surrounding herself with likeminded weirdos and geeks. Of course the first time she stumbled into another realm she would get decimated by rejection.

Retreat, retreat, retreat, her head warned her.

Advance, advance, advance, her heart said.

Not surprisingly her body was in league with her heart on this one. As she warmed herself against the hard length of Tristan beside her, Josie had to stop herself from purring. She could only be more content and catlike if someone dangled a toy mouse over her head for her to bat.

"Josie," Tristan whispered.

"Hmm," she said, closing her eyes to savor the moment before it went away.

"Did you just meow?"

Her eyes popped open. Had she? She had no idea, so probably. She sat up. "Let's eat food."

"As opposed to what?"

"As what opposed to what?" she said, frowning in confusion.

"You said let's eat food. What else would we eat?"

He was teasing her; she could tell from the miniscule modulation in his voice, from flat to almost flat. She stared down at him, teasing glint in her eye he couldn't begin to see. "If I said we could feast on love, would we starve?"

He waited a few beats and said, voice huskier than she'd ever heard it, "What do you think, Josie?"

"I have no idea," she answered honestly.

"Then I guess I have a better poker face than I thought," he said.

"Why are you so afraid to take off your mask with me?" she whispered. She sat up on her knees and eased closer. "I would be so careful with you; I would keep you safe." She rested her hand over his heart.

"It's not you I don't trust," he said, covering her hand over his heart.

Her other hand snaked out, brushing his brow. He closed his eyes, the expression on his face a mix of longing and tension. "Let's eat," she said softly.

He opened his eyes, gave a little nod, and followed her to the kitchen.

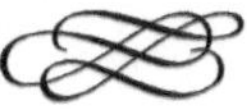

CHAPTER 22

"We need to go over everything again," Tristan said as they sat at the tiny table to eat the pre-made supper she'd reheated for them.

"This is pot roast. The cutlery is called silverware. You load it with the food and bring it to your lips." She demonstrated by placing some meat on her fork and taking a bite.

Tristan watched her, unsmiling and intent. "What fine lips they are," he noted, nudging her water closer when she choked.

"We're not well-suited, in the flirtation department," Josie said. "It's like seeing a weight, believing you have the strength to pick it up, then realizing you've made a horrible mistake and your spine is about to snap."

"I'm going to take that as a roundabout way of saying I make your spine tingle," Tristan said, stuffing a bit of roast between his lips as she laughed.

"What do we need to go over?" she asked.

"We're going to go back to the threat, but we need to widen the lens. You had just graduated. You and Gabe were at odds because he once again dumped you after prom. Your parents were together and working on their marriage. What else was happening in your world, with the people around you? Walk me through it." He took another bite and reached for his notebook, preparing to write.

Her brows rose. "You got shot and managed to maintain control of your notebook?"

"I'm really good," Tristan replied.

"It would have been super cool if the notebook stopped the bullet and saved you," Josie mused.

"Next time," he said.

"No next time," she said solemnly.

"No next time," he promised, as her eyes rounded with worry. His hand reached out, stroking her fingers and latching on when her hand unfurled and gave his a little squeeze. "Now take me back and walk me through."

Josie gave a little nod and let go of his hand, eyes going fuzzy with remembrance. "I had just graduated. Gabe and I were talking, but barely. I was pretty mad and he was full-throttle in denial about any misbehavior on his part. My summer job was getting ready to start."

Tristan frowned. "You didn't mention anything about a job before."

She shrugged. "It was just babysitting. For a while I worked at a drive through ice cream place, and I was ready for a change of pace."

"Who did you babysit for?"

"The Crawfords. I liked to consider myself a nanny, but they weren't rich and I wasn't well paid. I babysat fulltime, and it was a good distraction from my mental break. The kids kept me too occupied to be afraid or anxious, although we didn't get out as much that summer as they would have liked."

"Are they still around?"

"I don't know. My parents moved my sophomore year of college."

"Why?"

"Empty nest, downsizing. Though in retrospect they may have wanted the fresh start somewhere with no bad memories. My mom seemed happier after."

"Anything else going on with your friends?"

She shook her head. "Nothing that stands out."

"What about Bart and Janine?"

"Bart was finishing his CPA about that time. He thought he was big stuff, especially when he got his current job and started making good money."

"Did he have a girlfriend?"

"Almost always, no one of note."

"What about Janine?"

"Janine was finishing college. She got engaged to Keith around then." She frowned.

"What's the frown for? Is Keith the guy she married?"

"Married and divorced. That summer is kind of blurry for me, but now that I think back on it, I seem to remember her and Keith fighting a lot. It was a little surprising when they got engaged."

"What were they fighting about?"

"I don't know. Janine is five years older, years that have always mattered a lot to her. She keeps her own counsel, doesn't share secrets. I have no idea why she and Keith even got divorced, if I'm being honest."

"Did you like him?"

"I didn't hate him," Josie said carefully.

"That's not a ringing endorsement."

"I didn't know him that well. As I said, Janine and I weren't close. It was sort of like she kept him away from us, as if she either didn't want us to know him or want him to know us."

"Odd."

Josie shrugged. "Janine is odd."

"What was Bart's impression of him?"

"Pretty good, actually. He had this distinct way of speaking that Bart was good at mimicking."

He blinked at her. "I meant how did he view him, not how good was his literal impression of the guy."

"Oh," she said, cheeks going pink.

He stood, carefully set his napkin beside his plate, rounded the small table, and crouched beside her. Josie watched him curiously. He waited to speak until he was beside her. "I can't bend over the table in my current condition, but I needed to tell you I think you're about the cutest thing I have ever seen."

"Oh?" she asked, cheeks going pinker.

He nodded and took her hand, resting their joined hands on her lap. "I want to kiss you, all the time. Ridiculous amounts. Like, an unhealthy length of time. But I'm trying hard to focus, to keep my head in the game here. So if I seem…withdrawn to you, know it's because I'm trying to be, because I have to be."

"Oh," she said, nodding as she stared at their joined hands. He started to stand; she put her free hand on his shoulder and held him in place. "But why, though?"

"Why what?" he asked, eyes on her lips.

"Why do you feel the need to dissect your own heart that way, to keep everything separate?" Her hand eased to the side of his neck, stroking it gently. His breathing hitched, but his voice sounded normal when he answered.

"Because I need to think clearly. If I don't think clearly, I could mess up."

"What's the worst that could happen, if you mess up?" she asked, thumb smoothing over the ticking vein in his neck.

"Well, you could die," he said.

"That's much worse than anything I thought you were going to say," she said, and his cheek twitched. "But you know what's even worse than that?"

"Nothing?" he said.

She shook her head. "This half life you're leading. Not allowing yourself to feel, to laugh, to mess up and begin again. If I have to let go of my fear and start again, maybe you should, too." She faced him and rested both arms gently on his shoulders, careful not to put weight on his sore half.

"Who says I'm afraid?" he whispered.

"Your face, your voice, your refusal to reach out and touch me," she said.

"Maybe I just don't want to touch you," he said, which she might easily have taken as rejection, except that he was still there, kneeling beside her as if he couldn't pry himself away. And he was giving her the look, the hungry one she couldn't quantify, as if she were all the food in the world and he was starving.

"Do you?" she asked, holding perfectly still so she wouldn't break the moment and send him scurrying.

He stared at her a few beats, waging war with himself. "So much," he finally choked, hands reaching out to touch her waist. "So much, Josie, you have no idea. But…"

She shook her head. "Don't start with that." She eased forward and brushed her lips gently on his, shushing him. He tilted his head, angling to get closer as his hands gripped her waist, holding her in place as if she was the one who might disappear. He kissed her then, with so much pent-up longing she thought she might die for a minute, from the sensory overload.

And then, suddenly, they weren't alone.

CHAPTER 23

Gaines Hillcrest stood in the doorway, gun in hand, mouth partially ajar with shock and chagrin. "I knocked, and when no one answered it seemed like I should check."

Josie made an astonished "eep" of embarrassment and jutted an accusing finger toward Tristan. "He's a *really* good kisser."

"Thank you for letting me know," Gaines said as he holstered his gun. "You hope for the best when you hire someone, but there's no good way to ask during the interview."

Far from calming Josie, the statement increased her anxiety. She pressed her hands to her flushed cheeks. "Oh, no, you're his *boss*. Is he going to get fired for this?"

Tristan stood and gave her shoulder a reassuring squeeze. "Josie, you haven't been a client for six months, and I was your security guy, not your gym teacher."

She frowned up at him, now towering over her. "I'm distressed by how readily you had an inappropriate example lined up."

Beside them Gaines snorted a laugh. "You didn't tell me she was this funny."

"I didn't want to think or talk about her," Tristan replied.

"How's that working out?" Gaines asked with a grin.

"As well as ever," Tristan replied, sinking back into his seat with a sigh. "What's up?"

"The guy who shot you is…" Gaines darted Josie a glance and amended whatever he was going to say to, "no longer a threat."

"You arrested him already?" Josie said, scooting to the edge of her seat in excitement.

"Er…" Gaines hesitated, darting Tristan a glance for guidance.

"Cardiac arrested," Tristan said, giving her hand a squeeze.

Josie nodded, sitting back, while the two men continued.

"How'd you get him?" Tristan asked.

"Elyse tapped the cameras in the area, did some cross checking, wasn't too hard."

"They probably weren't expecting military intelligence to become involved," Tristan mused.

"Their mistake," Gaines said, grinning as he sat and surveyed the meal still on the table. "What? Jordan gave you pot roast? She made us eat leftover chili." He pinched a bite of roast and popped it in his mouth.

"At least now he's safely behind bars," Josie said.

The two men traded glances again. "Babe," Tristan said, resting his hand on her leg. "He's not in jail."

"But you said he's not a threat anymore," Josie said.

"He's not," Tristan returned. His expression didn't flicker, but somehow she got it now, clapping a hand over her mouth to stifle her gasp.

"He's dead?" she said in a shaky whisper.

"Or *really* good at pretending," Gaines said, stealing another bite of roast.

"Someone is dead because of me? Because of my case?"

"Nah," Gaines said. "This guy was a pro. If this case hadn't gotten him, something else would."

"So you offed him vigilante style? Like a ninja assassin?" Josie asked, staring at Gaines with a combination of horror and fascination that made him choke back another laugh.

"Josie, no, of course not. I'm a private citizen now. I can't work outside the law."

Tristan choked.

"Technically," Gaines amended. "It's a fine line, lots of wiggle room. But this was clear-cut. My IT person found the guy, and I handed everything over to the local police. They went to pick the guy up, ask a few questions, and got into a shootout. The good guys won, the bad guy lost. It's very Wild West." Gaines gave up the pretense of pinching bites and appropriated Tristan's plate, adding more meat and potatoes to it.

Josie's mind felt sluggish, as if she were playing catch up with information the men had already assimilated. "So Tristan is safe now?"

Tristan and Gaines did the thing where they looked at each other again, trying to figure out how to break it to her. Tristan leaned closer. "Josie, I was always safe. *I* was never the target."

Josie's mouth froze in an "O" of understanding.

"Along those lines, I brought a picture, in case you might recognize him."

Josie reached out her hand, then drew it back again. "Is there going to be a lot of blood?"

Gaines tipped his head, studying her. "Do you think I brought you a picture of his death?"

"Well, now I don't," Josie said, wrinkling her nose at him when he sputtered another laugh.

"Josie, you're good to have around, girl," Gaines said. He handed her the picture and tucked into his food.

Tristan leaned closer, studying the picture, too. "Is it the guy who made the threat?" he asked, trying to snuff hope out of his words. If it was the man who'd made the threat, they could wrap everything up with a neat little bow.

Josie shook her head. "This guy is too young, and the hair and eyes are all wrong. Yeesh, he looks *so* young. How does a guy this young get to be a hired killer? And he looks so normal. I expected, I don't know, a snarl and neck tattoos or something. He's so clean cut."

"The best assassins blend," Gaines noted. "I knew this woman, she's retired now, but back in the day she was crazy good, could get next to anyone by never standing out."

Josie blinked at him, hands gripping the picture. "There are women who kill people?"

"Um, no, of course not," Gaines said, dropping his eyes to his plate as he resumed stuffing food.

Josie faced Tristan. "Do you know women who kill people?"

"Not in the literal sense," he said.

"What does that mean?" she asked.

"It means some women make men feel like they're dead when they go away." He leaned forward and pressed his lips to her neck, pausing to inhale.

"I should have known flirting from you would involve assassins," Josie said, remembering they still had an audience when Gaines snorted and coughed.

"Anyway," Gaines said, clearing his throat. "I think it's safe to leave here, but be wary. In the meantime, I have Elyse digging at the whisper network, tugging at threads to see if she can figure out who posted the original answer to your question."

"Thank you," Josie said. Her tone was normal, but she was still gripping the picture of the dead assassin.

"Josie, he made a mistake by making a move. We're going to get this figured out," Gaines assured her.

"And in the meantime, you'll be safe," Tristan added.

"Okay, but..." Josie began but trailed off.

"But what?" Tristan asked, giving her leg a reassuring squeeze.

"Could we maybe not tell Jordan this is over so she'll continue to cook for us?" Josie suggested.

"Now that I know she's giving you the good stuff while I get left-overs, I'm going to tell her it's still going and keep the good stuff for myself," Gaines said.

"You're a monster," Josie told him.

"If you're going to run with the big dogs, Josie, you're going to have to bring it up to our level," Gaines said, using the fork to point between himself and Tristan.

Josie set aside the picture she'd been clutching and sat a little straighter. "You may be a SEAL turned spy, turned security expert, Gaines, but have you ever faced a room of five year olds when the full moon fell on the same day as trick-or-treat?"

Gaines put up his hands in surrender. "You win, Josie, I can't compete with that."

"This calls for a celebratory lozenge," Josie said. Reaching in her pocket, she withdrew the tin, opened it, and placed one in Tristan's waiting mouth.

"I'm glad I came," Gaines said, eyeing them. "This has been a *very* informative outing. I am learning so much about my taciturn employee."

"He's taciturn with you, too? I thought it was only me," Josie said, now also eyeing Tristan.

"If this is your definition of taciturn, I'd say you don't know the meaning," Gaines said, noting their cozy side-by-side position, along with Tristan's hand on her leg.

"I'm going to take comfort in the fact that he doesn't sit like this with you," Josie said, handing Gaines a napkin when he laughed and spewed the water he'd been sipping.

After turning off the boat's generator and checking the perimeter, Gaines took his leave, and so did Tristan and Josie.

"This is a sign of my devotion, Josie," Tristan told her as he buckled himself in the passenger seat of her car. "That I'm riding with you, instead of him."

"Be still my heart," Josie said, tossing him a smile as she put the car into reverse.

"Let's hope mine keeps beating, despite the coming nightmare," Tristan said, gripping the edge of the seat and closing his eyes.

"Tristan, we're here."

Either despite or because of his passenger anxiety, Tristan fell asleep almost as soon as they were on the road. Josie enjoyed the opportunity to truck along as slowly as she pleased, ignoring the people who swerved, honked and jabbed various body parts in her direction in protest. She woke him only when they were safely in her driveway. Knowing Tristan, she guessed he wouldn't want to stay with her, would feel like it was presuming too much for her to care for him. But she was prepared to argue and be firm on this point: Tristan needed a keeper, at least for the time being. Who better than Josie, who had nothing else to do?

His eyes flicked open, boring into hers. "Josie," he began.

She put up a hand. "You're staying with me. I don't want to hear any argument."

"Josie," he said, voice raspier.

"What?" she asked, ready to lay out her list of arguments she'd prepared on the drive home.

"I think I might be sick."

Suddenly she noted his intense paleness. "Oh." She touched a hand to his clammy cheek, giving it an affectionate press. "Let's get you inside."

She was too small to be much help, but she came around for moral support, at the very least, propping herself under his arm and attempting to take some of his weight as she herded him toward the house. She deposited him next to the bathroom where he gave her a little shove and slammed the door, one she didn't take offense at. No one wanted a companion in there.

Anxious to be of assistance, she retrieved a few items and waited until he emerged, slipping back under his arm and shepherding him to her guest room. Despite never having a guest, she had put a lot of care and thought into the room. Some dim corner of her brain was pleased by that forethought now as she held the covers for Tristan, tucking him in to the cool, clean, and new sheets she had lovingly selected.

After he was properly arranged, she perched on the edge of the bed, placed a cool cloth on his head, and presented him with a glass of ginger ale, a plate of saltine crackers, and a large bowl for, "Just in case."

Tristan blinked at her with his usual expression, too-big eyes, serious and intent.

"What's that look for?" she asked softly, smoothing her hand over the cloth on his forehead. She had already discerned he was more apt to answer her questions when his defenses were down. Was it wrong to use that against him? Yes. Did she care? Not even a little.

"No one has ever taken care of me when I'm sick," he admitted.

Her hand paused, the weight of that settling against her heart with a hard jab. "Never ever?"

He shook his head.

"Then I guess I have a lot to make up for. What can I get you?"

"Nothing."

"Really nothing, or I-don't-want-to-be-a-bother nothing?"

"I don't actually know," he said slowly. "This is all new to me."

"Let's try this: does anything sound good, anything at all? Is there anything that might make you feel better in this moment?"

"There's one thing," he said slowly, hesitantly.

"What is it?" she asked.

"Will you lie next to me?"

She had expected something tangible—a glass of lemonade, a peppermint. Companionship was something unexpected. Tristan seemed more like the kind of guy who wanted to be left alone when he didn't feel well, but maybe he wasn't. Maybe he liked being coddled and petted but had no idea how to go about making it happen. Because it never had before. How was that possible? Didn't he have a mother or grandmother?

Josie moved the just-in-case bowl to the other side of the bed, then lay down, stretching the length of him, letting her warmth ooze into him. She took his hand and gave it a squeeze, smoothing her thumb over his fingers, and then deposited a kiss on his shoulder.

They lay in peaceful silence for a long time, so long that Josie thought he had fallen asleep. She was almost there herself when he spoke. "Who took care of you when you were sick?"

"Usually my mom, but sometimes Bart. One time when I was about five I got really sick, some kind of virus that lasted for days and had a high fever. That must have been during the bad time with my parents because I don't remember my mom being there. I remember Bart, sleeping beside my bed, handing me popsicles and suckers, frowning as he checked my temperature." She paused. "I'd forgotten about that, or maybe blocked it out. He must have been so freaked out, only a kid himself and trying to care for a sick five year old."

They lay in silence a while longer before she chanced a question of her own. "Why did no one take care of you?"

"Not that kind of family," Tristan said. "It was more of a kill or be killed situation, like enemy combatants. Never peaceful or nurturing."

"I'm very sorry," Josie said, giving his hand a squeeze.

He swallowed hard, and when his voice spoke, it was raspy. "I'm not a safe bet, Josie, on a number of levels."

She twisted to stare up at him, but he kept his gaze on the ceiling. Her hand reached out, pressing against his forehead. "Sometimes the riskiest bets have the biggest payouts."

He finally looked at her. She could tell he wanted to smile, could read it in his eyes. His lips remained firmly locked together, however.

She nudged him. "What does it take to get you to let loose and give in to a smile?"

"I'll let you know," he said. He rolled onto his side and slid his hand over her waist, urging her to curve herself against him, which she did as naturally as breathing.

"Smiling is out but spooning is in?" she said.

"Spooning is always in when it's with you," he returned.

"I think that was supposed to be flattering, but instead it sounds like you went through a whole lot of people to try and find someone spoonable."

He didn't reply. She finally twisted to see his face. Either he was asleep, or he was really good at faking. A minute later, Josie was definitely asleep.

In the morning they woke face to face, hands pillowed beneath their cheeks, eyes on each other. Josie had no idea how long Tristan had been awake, but it seemed like a while, if the bright-eyed way he stared at her was any indication.

"How are you feeling?" she whispered. There was no reason to whisper, except a pressing need to not disturb the early morning stillness and possibly whatever little spell felt woven around them in this moment.

"Good."

"Regular good or Tristan good?" she asked. The way he stared at her made her heart thump, her words breathless.

"What's the difference?" he asked, easing closer so only a whisper separated them, their noses almost but not quite touching.

"Regular people don't get shot and keep functioning," she said, fingers latching onto his shirt, anchoring him in place.

"I'm feeling Josie good," he said.

"What's that?"

"It's the way I feel when I'm near you, like anything is possible." He cupped her chin and brushed his lips on hers. Josie felt tingly, also from the possibility of what could be, as much as from what already was. She had never considered anyone like Tristan before, never believed anyone like Tristan would consider her. She had spent her adolescence trying on different personas, until she found the one that fit best. Since then she had settled into "quirky kindergarten teacher" with aplomb, believing it was who she was, who she was meant to be. What if there was more? What if there was Tristan?

Tristan was different than anything that came before. It wasn't just that he had an exciting job and big muscles, although she was honest enough to admit those things intrigued her. She had always leaned more cerebral in her dating choices. Tristan's intellect may not be the first thing that jumped out at her, but he was *smart*. She could see it in his eyes as he took in information and pieced it together.

The thing about Tristan that snared her, more than anything else, was his wildness. Tristan was uncontained and unpredictable, but in the best possible way. Before, when she tried to date Tony, he'd had that same sort of wildness that excited her. But even as a kid she'd sensed the danger in his brand of wildness, knew it had the capacity to wound and damage her in irreparable ways. Tristan wasn't like that, and all of a sudden she understood the difference. She *trusted* Tristan. True, she had no idea what he would do next, couldn't begin to predict his thoughts or actions. But beneath his toughness she saw his soft and tender side. Tristan, for all his word economy and emotional reserve, had cared for her in a way no one else ever had, not even her family. He had studied her, assessed the things her heart needed to hear, and made it his mission to help her heal, to become whole. He hadn't tried to change her, hadn't tried to diminish her or force her to contain her too-big emotions, like everyone who came before. Instead he seemed to be trying to help her become the best possible version of herself, the full Josie. As if he wanted more of her, not less. As if he could see all she could become and wanted to help her get there. It blew her mind a little, that realization, that Tristan wanted more of her, not less. The first person in her entire life to do so. And it begged the question, *How can I do the same for him in return?* How could she help him become more Tristan, not less?

"The way you're looking at me," Tristan whispered, brushing his finger on her cheek.

"How am I looking at you?" she whispered. Was she so transparent?

"Like I'm not a banged up ex-cop who hasn't showered in three days."

She smiled. "You are a little stinky."

He winced, drawing back. "Sorry."

"Never said I didn't like it," she said, chasing his lips with hers.

"You can't possibly."

"Wrong. It's manly. Like Tristan, but more. Tristan 2.0: holier, sweatier, and…" She left it hanging, hoping he would take the bait.

"And?"

"Smilier."

"Two out of three ain't bad," he murmured, planting his hand possessively on her hip to draw her closer. She gladly complied, wriggling and nestling against him, sliding her hands around his neck.

"Josie." His whisper was fervent, but ruined by the loud growl of his stomach.

She laughed and pressed her forehead to his shoulder.

"I stink and I have no game," he lamented.

"You're doing all right," she assured him.

His hand smoothed over her head, and he kissed her forehead. "You still going to like me if I shower the stink away?"

"I think it's safe to say it's more than stink deep at this point," Josie said.

Tristan's eyes flashed with…something. Josie wasn't versed enough in his type to understand what it was, but it looked like something good, something she wanted more of.

"Are you okay to shower? You're not going to keel over?" She petted his head, newly concerned over his unaccustomed fragility.

Tristan closed his eyes, leaning into her touch. "I'll be fine."

"I'll make breakfast while you do that. Please leave the door cracked, in case of emergency."

"You don't have to fuss," he said, but the way he gripped her tighter told her he liked it when she fussed. Probably a lot. *No one has ever taken care of me before.* Those words would haunt her forever, she thought.

"I *like* to fuss," she assured him. She eased away. His hand reached for her and he groaned.

"If one of us doesn't go, we're going to stay here all day," she said.

"You make that seem like a bad thing," he said, sitting up slowly, painfully.

Josie watched, swallowing hard. Even wounded and bedraggled he was a sight. So handsome and powerful, like a sleek tiger.

"Josie," he said. Just that, and it amazed her how many different ways he could say her name. This one was intent, and a little cocky.

"I didn't know eyes could smolder like that," she said, clasping her hands behind her back with sudden nerves.

"Come back here, I'll show you what else they can do," he said.

When Josie made a "meep" sound and darted out of the room, she could almost swear she heard him laughing behind her.

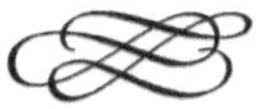

CHAPTER 25

"I have nothing to wear." Tristan made the announcement as he eased into the kitchen and sat down with a pained sigh.

"I'd say you could borrow something of mine, but I'd probably need to piece five things together, and my sewing skills are not up to par." She gave his bicep a little squeeze. "Do you want me to go to the store and get something for you?"

"I thought we could go to my apartment, pick a few things up."

She blinked at him.

He paused, forkful of food halfway to his mouth. "What?"

"I get to see the inner sanctum?"

"Such as it is. Please keep your expectations grounded in reality," he warned.

"Okay," she said, but she fizzed with anticipation. Tristan was so guarded; she never imagined that he would let her see where he slept.

"Maybe we can also stop by work," he suggested.

"Sure," she agreed, almost wriggling with excitement now.

Josie had made a feast; eggs, bacon, toast, and juice, but Tristan had a hard time focusing on anything but her. True, she was adorable, today wearing a shirt covered in iridescent dragonflies, her hair piled in a haphazard messy bun. But it was her absolute ease with life, the joy with which she embraced the mundane that captivated him. There should be no reason his job or apartment inspired any emotion other than boredom, but Josie saw it as some grand adventure, probably saw all of life that way, and it was a pleasure for Tristan to absorb her excitement secondhand. For Tristan, who preferred to filter all of his emotions before he allowed himself to express them, it was a handy relay system. Josie could feel all the feels he viewed as weakness in himself, and he could take vicarious pleasure through her unbridled enthusiasm.

"Thank you for breakfast," he said, eyes fastened on her.

"You're welcome," she said, eyes fastened on him. "It's nice to have a reason to cook. Usually I subsist on cereal."

"And yet you have ingredients on hand to whip up a full breakfast," he noted.

"Maybe it's a girl thing," she suggested with a shrug.

"It's not," Tristan declared. He had never known a woman—either in his family or among the women he'd dated—who could assemble and cook a meal at a moment's notice. It was part of her Josieness, and one of the things that made them fundamentally different. Josie knew how to make a house a home. What Tristan didn't know was if those differences between them were insurmountable. He had believed so, at first, and strived to keep his distance. But now... Were they able to find a middle ground, or did he want her so much he no longer cared?

He reached for her hand and gave it a squeeze. "Do you think Bart would be willing to meet us for lunch while we're downtown?"

She blinked, reorienting herself. Clearly she hadn't thought her brother would be drawn into the mix today, but Tristan was anxious to find answers, to tie up Josie's case and make her safe.

"I can try." She let go of his hand and reached for her phone, sending her brother a text.

He responded almost immediately, before she could set her phone aside. "Bart says yes. Reading between the lines and the speed of his response, I'd say he has some questions of his own for me, namely why you're involved again." Her eyes flicked to him, worried now.

"Bart can be, you know, he can be intense, when he's worried about me. He's protective like that."

"I'm not afraid of your brother," Tristan said easily. "Besides, Bart and I are on the same side here. We're both team Josie."

"You should get matching shirts," Josie said, pointing her fork at him. "Like a bowling team. Something neon, with your name over the pocket."

"You'd love that, wouldn't you?" he said.

"You know it," she agreed happily. They finished their meal in pleasant silence. Tristan offered to help clean up, but she waved him away. He contented himself instead by watching her, absorbing the peaceful scene in her cozy kitchen. His apartment would be stark contrast after this, so much that he began to dread going back. If not for the want of his clothes and razor, he might be content to never leave this place. *Team Josie for life.* He rested his head on his fist, blinking sleepily at her as she washed the dishes and wiped the stove, tidying everything, making it neat and perfect once more.

"Ready?" she asked, after she set the sponge aside for the final time, then, "What?"

"Nothing," he said, which was momentarily true because he was speechless. He often felt speechless in her presence, a potent yearning so strong and powerful it knocked him breathless and robbed him of the words that could express and articulate what was happening.

"Are you ready to go?" she asked.

"Yes," he said, and it came out more clipped than he'd intended.

Her eyes turned wary. "Are you regretting inviting me to your pad?"

"Josie." He crooked his finger at her.

Slowly she went forward, until she was within reach. Then he drew her closer, cinching her against him with an arm around her waist. "Yes," she said, feeling a little breathless herself now.

"No one has said the word 'pad' to describe someone's apartment since Major Nelson let Jeannie out of the bottle." He rested his head on her stomach, sighing in contentment.

"Tristan," Josie said.

"Hmm." He closed his eyes and inhaled, drawing her Josie scent into his nostrils.

"Spoiler alert: I don't do things like other people." She kissed the top of his head.

He tipped his face back. "No. You do them better. I like your Josieness."

"Yeah?" she said, cheeks heating with pleasure.

"So much," he affirmed, hand cupping her cheek. "The Josier, the better."

"No one has ever made my name so many parts of speech before," she said. Her phone rang and, distracted, she reached for it by habit and froze.

"Your mom?" Tristan guessed.

"Eli. He never calls, he always texts. I sort of forgot to call him back after I ran out on him when Gaines contacted me."

"You should answer it," Tristan said, and not even he could define the odd energy in his tone.

"Okay," Josie said and took a shaky breath. "Hello."

"Josie, hey, hi. Are you okay?"

"Yes."

"Um…I ask because you answered your phone, turned four shades of white, sprinted to your car, and sped away. As one does, of course. And then ignores all calls and texts and in-person appearances thereafter."

"Eli, I am so sorry. The phone call turned out to be about Tristan."

"Tristan? Did he get married? Did you go try to stop his wedding? Were you successful? Because I've never actually seen that in person. Not going to lie, I'd be sorry to miss it."

She laughed, angling away from Tristan when he frowned. "Yes, and the wedding was in Tijuana, so obviously I got arrested, and then there was that bogus drug charge. Long story short, how much cash can you liquidate by tomorrow?"

"You're assuming I don't have tons of cash already on hand. Did I not tell you about my Beanie Baby collection? I thought we'd been over this."

Josie snorted a laugh again, feeling the ball of stress that had been in her chest slip away. Eli had always been able to make her laugh, it was one of her favorite things about him.

"Are you okay, for real?" he asked. "And how is Tristan? He's not, like, dead or something, is he?"

She shuddered, not even liking the thought. "No, he but he did get shot."

There was a significant pause. "Really? Is that still part of the bit?"

"No, that part was real. I was his emergency contact, so I had to go to the hospital and sign papers."

"Was he that bad off that he couldn't sign his own papers?"

"He was unconscious from the fall." She angled back toward Tristan who was watching her with one eyebrow quirked. How bad was his head wound? She had forgotten the concussion, in light of the gunshot, but in the scheme of things a concussion was probably worse.

"Off a waterfall? Like Sherlock?"

"Exactly like Sherlock," she said, smiling when Tristan rolled his eyes. She reached out a hand, touching his head, and he tilted, leaning into her gentle ministration.

"Do you need anything? Are you still at the hospital?" Eli asked.

Josie dropped her hand, feeling the knife of guilt twist a little. Eli was so good and thoughtful, had been such a caring friend to her the last few months. And they had been heading toward more, even if neither of them had addressed the elephant in the room.

"No, I'm home. We got here last night." She squeezed her eyes closed at the pause on the other end of the line.

"He's at your house?"

"He's in need of some care. A sizeable chunk of him is missing now." And he had a head wound. How had she forgotten that? She kissed her finger and touched it gently to his head. He took her finger and kissed it, tossing her a wink that made her a little weak kneed and swoony.

"To be fair, he had a lot to begin with, so…" Eli paused and cleared his throat. Josie could hear his skin rasp, as if he was chafing his hand over it. "Listen, I know this is crazy selfish of me, but I was wondering if you're still going to be able to make my cousin's wedding on Saturday."

Josie smacked herself upside the head. She had forgotten. "Yes, of course," she blurted, turning away from Tristan again when he shook his head in disagreement. "Barring any emergency."

"I guess I should have asked how many people have you listed as their emergency contact before we made plans. The falafel guy who has your number first on his list might get hit by a train, for instance." Josie laughed, nervously this time, because he sounded a little peeved.

"Not going to happen. Jorge is terrified of trains," she replied, and now it was Eli's turn to laugh. "I'm sorry I ditched you and disappeared. It's been an eventful couple of days. If for some reason I think I can't make the wedding, I'll try to give you as much lead time to find another date as possible."

"Oh, yeah, lead time. That's what it takes for me to score a date," Eli said dryly. "All of high school and college, I was just missing lead time. Turns out I should have told them in preschool I was available."

Josie laughed hard, the genuine and deep sort of laugh Eli could evoke. "If I have to ditch, I will find you another date, how's that?"

"Josie, I am not taking Tristan, I don't care how he fills out a tuxedo," Eli said, and Josie bent over, pressing her hand to her stomach.

"Stop it, you're making my nose run. I'll talk to you as soon as things calm down here a little. We're running errands today."

"Promise me you're not going to look for Tristan's missing piece. Contrary to the cartoons we've watched, you can't actually put people back together like that."

"Eli, stop it," Josie wailed swiping her teary eyes. She said goodbye and tossed the phone on her table, realizing as she did so that the levity left the room with Eli's voice. Tristan now stared at her, looking imposing and severe.

"So," he said. "How is good old Eli?"

"He's very Eli," Josie said, which was a reasonable thing to say about someone you had known since middle school. Eli was just Eli, like the weather. He was unchanging, and she liked it that way.

"You have a date."

"What? No."

"A wedding."

She waved him away. "It's just his cousin's wedding. You know how things like that are. No one wants to go to a family wedding alone. All those people sidling up to make snide remarks about when it's going to be your turn." She grimaced, remembering one too many family weddings of her own like that.

"Josie, that's the literal definition of a date."

She tossed her hands in annoyance. "Fine, it's a date. But it's not a *date* date. It's an Eli date."

"He wants it to be more, and you know it."

"I can't control what he wants," she said hotly.

"And what do you want?"

"I…" She started to answer, realized she couldn't, and blinked at him in confusion.

His expression turned to stone. "You cannot go."

Now her face matched his. "What do you mean I can't go? You can't tell me what to do."

"I'm your security guard, the one who was shot by the person who wants to kill you. It's not safe."

"He's had a decade to take me out, it's not going to happen at a friend's wedding," she said.

"You don't know that."

"Neither do you. I'm not going to stop living my life."

"Fine, then I'll go with you."

She rolled her eyes. "You can't go with me on a date."

He jutted a finger in her direction. "You said it's not a date."

She jutted a finger in return. "You said it is. And why do you care? Really, Tristan, why? I went to your office. I told you I wanted to see you. You threw me out."

"I did not throw you out, I would never throw you out."

"Really? Because I remember landing on my butt and bouncing a couple of times in pain and humiliation," she said, tears stinging her eyes. His rejection had hurt her. Badly.

"Josie," he said, sounding like he was in agony. He reached out, snagged her shirt, and tugged her against him. "It was never about not wanting you, not for one second. Did you think that?"

Her cheeks were flushed, with a combination of his proximity and embarrassment. "What was I to think?"

His hand stroked her warm cheek. "I want you," he said, drawing a ragged breath. "I wanted you then, I want you now. With every part of me, even the one that got shot away. I just want." His fingers slid to her chin, tilting it toward him, and then he kissed her, an all-in burst of passion that was simultaneously too much and not enough. Neither was certain if he pulled Josie into his lap or she went of her own accord. Maybe it was him, because his fist was tangled in her shirt, his thumb brushing her bare navel, sending sparks of delirious heat all the way to her fingers and toes.

Josie was the one to regain a tiny modicum of sanity. She pushed against his shoulders and found a whisper of space, enough to ask a question. "Why, then?"

He paused and blinked at her, panting and dazed. "What?"

She took a breath and gained a half inch of space. "If I wanted you, and you wanted me, why did you say no? Why did you reject me?"

Now Tristan was the one to ease back. He licked his lips. "Because I…" And there the words stuck. As hard as he tried, they wouldn't come.

Josie stared at him, confusion turning to pain. Why wouldn't he tell her? Clearly he was going through something, but why wouldn't he fight for her?

The thumb on her stomach, once so promising, now felt like a bruise. She tugged his hand away, kissed the thumb, and tucked it against his chest. Then she stood and smoothed her rumpled visage.

"We should go. I'll be in the car."

"I think I can drive."

Her head snapped up, eyes dancing fire, hands landing on her hips. "It's my car, and these are my rules, and you will be the passenger. Now I'll *be in the car.*"

She turned and swept from the house. Tristan waited until she was well and truly gone to snort a laugh and press his hand over his eyes. Gone, he was totally and completely gone.

CHAPTER 26

Tristan's apartment seemed even worse, in comparison to Josie's house. Cold, sterile, and gray, it was uncomfortable at the best of times. With Josie herself in attendance, it was like someone captured a rainbow in a plastic bubble and set it in the middle of his living room in order to make a point. One of these things is warm and alive, the other is not. His apartment was not.

"You're so tidy," Josie said, squeezing his bicep. Driving had worked to release whatever irritation she held at him, so she was remarkably cheerful and upbeat by the time they arrived at his apartment, a portion of a house in the slummy part of DC.

"You don't have to bright side my lackluster dwelling," Tristan told her, but that only worked to make her smile harder.

"Lackluster dwelling. Do you know your vocabulary increases relative to the size of your nervous discomfort? If I stand here long enough, you're going to switch to Latin."

Ignoring her, a task that was nearly impossible because she was the only color and light in the room, he turned his back on her and tried to see the space through her eyes. One used and beige loveseat, check. A beaten up fake wood table and lone wobbly chair, check. "It looks like the serial killer starter package," he noted.

"But it's so *clean*," Josie blurted, linking her arm with his.

Tristan stared down at the top of her head while she scanned his apartment, somehow finding joy in the Spartan accommodation. "Do you want to see the bedroom?" he asked.

"You even have to ask?" she said, tipping her face up toward his. Whatever she saw made her freeze and blink, throat bobbing as she swallowed hard.

He took her hand and tugged her forward, toward the only other room in the dilapidated excuse for a living space, his tiny bedroom.

It was dark, with one lone light overhead and a window air conditioner sucking up any chance for sunlight. But, as she'd noted, it was clean. The sheets were fresh, the bed was made, the floor swept, and everything he owned put away and out of sight. Tristan thought about Josie's guest room, overflowing with color, pattern, texture, and warmth and thought this was perhaps the dumpiest, most depressing room in the history of rooms. Josie, transversely, slid her arms around his waist and gave him a reassuring hug.

"You're a minimalist."

"You're a maximalist," he said, sliding his good arm around her and giving her a squeeze.

She tipped her head up to see him again, this time smiling in amusement. "How did you hear that word?"

"My barber apparently subscribes to a house decorating magazine. They had an in-depth article on the maximalist movement. Reminded me of you." Then again, what hadn't reminded him of her every minute of the last six months?

"Is that a polite way of calling me a hoarder?" she asked.

"It's a true way of saying you have a talent for personalizing every space and making it homey, of making it your own." He, on the other hand, hadn't bought towels for the first month he lived here, only remembering his lack when he had to air dry after every shower.

"Must be another one of those girl things."

"Nope. I've known a lot of women, not all of them had that talent."

Josie fixed her gaze on him, thinking. "Define 'a lot' for me."

He sighed. "A lot, Josie. Probably exactly what you're thinking."

"Hmm," she said, aiming for neutrality and failing greatly.

It was hard to defend himself when that was her only comment, not that he would know what to say anyway. He could feel her pulling away again, understood that she thought this was the problem between them, those nameless, faceless others. If only he could explain to her the difference between her and them, between then and now, but that would mean explaining everything else. That was something he couldn't do.

"We should go. We don't want to keep Bart waiting," Josie said. She leaned against the jamb while Tristan quickly packed a bag, and then they went to his office.

"Hey, Josie. How's the caretaking going?" Gaines asked as soon as they stepped into the office.

"Not so well. I can't remember how to tie the sort of knots that will let me keep him contained enough to heal," Josie lamented.

"If you think it takes knots to keep a man, you're doing it wrong," Gaines returned.

"I think I might be too young to hear that joke," Josie said, pressing her hands over her ears.

Gaines laughed. "Careful. If you linger here too long, I'll put you to work."

Josie perked up, which seemed impossible since she was already bright and perky. "Really? I would love that. Please, load me up." She held out her arms.

Gaines, happy to comply, gave her enough work to last the week, a mix of filing, accounting, and highlighting a transcript from one of his cases.

"This is so awesome. I feel like Miss Moneypenny."

"I guess that makes Tristan James Bond and me M. I'll take it," Gaines said, giving her a little salute as he returned to his office.

Instead of remaining in the lobby at the desk they had set up for the secretary they didn't yet have, Josie followed Tristan into his office, spreading her work on the unused portion of his desk. He didn't call her on it because he was happy to have her there. Unlike most people, who drained his batteries, he enjoyed being with Josie.

She lightened something inside him. Her passive company, even as she did busywork, lessened his loneliness and made him feel more alive, less like a robot going through the motions of living. With Josie it was easy to believe he could be a real person who embraced life, with all its sticky emotions and difficult circumstances. On his own he sometimes felt as if he was stuck in a neutral cycle of existence, waiting for the next thing. *Josie is the next thing,* he thought.

"What?" she asked, and he realized he was staring at her.

"I like to have you here," he said honestly. She made him feel like he could be candid and vulnerable and she would keep that vulnerable part of him safe. He had never had that with anyone else, male or female.

"I like to be here," she said, cheeks flushing with uncharacteristic shyness.

"You could stay full time. Come be our intern." He wagged his brows.

"As intriguing as that thought is, I think I'm where I'm supposed to be. You wouldn't believe how many kids need a stable and loving adult influence in their lives."

"Yeah, I would," he said, reaching out to cup her cheek. "And you're exactly where you need to be. But maybe we can steal you sometimes, Moneypenny."

"You could probably get me to do anything, with a cool nickname," Josie said. "Within reason," she added, when his eyebrows shot to his hairline.

They worked in companionable silence a while, until Bart arrived, along with their lunch, a delivery from a local sandwich shop.

"Tristan," Bart greeted him from the doorway, looking as squinty and suspicious as Josie had guessed he would. "This is a surprise. We haven't heard from you in a while." He darted Josie a glance, probably checking to see if she was in a heartbroken puddle. She had tried hard to hide the pain of Tristan's rejection from her family, but she wasn't certain she succeeded with Bart, who had always taken her heartache too personally.

"We bought you a turkey club," Josie blurted, nervously smoothing her hair when Bart continued to assess her. "I hope that's okay."

"I'm not picky," Bart said. He eased into the room and sat, but his movement was a study in forced casualness, as if he was trying hard to fuse an emotion, or lack thereof, into his features.

He sat and adjusted the cuffs of his shirt, pulling them from beneath his suit jacket, and then he spoke. "What is this about? I thought Tristan was out of the picture? Why are you here? And why are you working?" He frowned at the obvious stack of work in front of Josie.

"We eloped and I quit my job to be with Tristan fulltime," Josie said.

Bart's jaw dropped, but before he could gear up for an angry retort, Josie put up a hand to halt him.

"I thought it best to name your worst suspicion and get it out of the way. Of course that's not what happened. Tristan met with a little misfortune, and I've been helping him get a few things squared away. I would never elope with someone I'm not even seeing, and I would never quit my job because, despite anything you might believe to the contrary, I am a sensible and productive adult."

Bart took in a breath, held it a few beats, and let it out slowly before speaking, giving himself time to frame a response. "You are that. But you're also my little sister, and it's my job to worry about you, to make sure you're staying on track."

Tristan had watched the exchange without comment, in the way Josie had become accustomed to, as if he was seeing beneath the surface and taking mental notes on undertones she didn't yet comprehend. When he spoke, she sat back and listened, letting him take the lead.

"You take that job seriously," he said. He took a bite of his sandwich, letting the comment hang.

"You know I do," Bart said. It was clear he hadn't yet decided if Tristan was friend or foe, where Josie was concerned. Had he broken his sister's heart? Would he still, if given the chance?

Josie split her pickle in two and gave half to each man, purposely bridging the gap between them with dill. She wanted to show Bart she wasn't wounded, that she liked and trusted Tristan. It must have worked, at least a little, because he picked up his half of the pickle and took a bite, relaxing the stiff set of his shoulders a little.

"You've been doing it a long time," Tristan continued into the lingering silence.

Bart gave a nod, a little furrow working between his brows. Josie remained silent, letting Tristan work, uncertain where he was going.

"Like the night Tony died," Tristan said after another bite.

Bart froze, sandwich halfway to his mouth, bacon dangling precariously from the side. "What?" He set the sandwich aside.

"Something has been missing from that story from the beginning. It was too neat, too orderly. You confronted Tony after the party."

Josie remained silent and wide-eyed, but she accidentally squeezed her sandwich too hard, forcing cheese and mayonnaise to shoot between her fingers. With a sigh, Bart reached for a napkin, then reached for Josie's hand and began to clean the mess, as he had when she was a child.

"Gabe called me from the party. He told me Josie and Tony were fighting, that Tony was drunk and trying to get Josie in the car with him. He was going to physically stop her from getting in the car, if it came to it, but it wasn't necessary. Tony left, and Josie remained. I was already on my way to pick her up when the little punk blew past me. I was mad, thinking of the danger he might have put her in. So I did a uey and followed him."

Josie gasped and bit her lip. Bart gave her a tight little smile and finished cleaning her hand.

"What happened?" Tristan prompted.

"He pulled over. We got out of our cars. I confronted him, told him he wasn't allowed to see Josie anymore and to leave her alone."

"What was his response to that?" Tristan asked.

"Not worth repeating," Bart said, shaking his head. "It was a tense, volatile exchange. Not going to lie, I was ready to punch him, to lay him flat, but it never happened. He got in his car and sped away."

"And then?" Tristan asked.

"I stared after him for a bit, contemplating whether or not I wanted to follow and drive home my point, or drive my fist in his face. I was mad, not only at him, but at myself for being so easily duped by him. I thought he was a good choice for Josie, and then it turned out he was a drunken, violent loser. Plus I was young and full of protective machismo." He shrugged. "I didn't go after him." He paused and looked away, toward the window. "Not even when I heard the crash. I guessed what had happened. He was so drunk, it wasn't hard to put two and two together. I didn't check on him, didn't call it in. Instead I got in my car and headed back to the party for Josie. Maybe if I would have..." he let the thought trail.

Tristan shook his head. "Wouldn't have made a difference. From everything I read, he was dead on impact. Absolutely nothing would have saved him. My only concern was that you weren't the one chasing him, the one who ran him off the road."

Bart shook his head. "I didn't, but not because I didn't want to. And, as much guilt as I've felt for not checking on him or calling for help, I wasn't sad he died. Not even a little." His glance darted to Josie again, reassuring himself she was alive and okay.

"Then let go of the guilt," Tristan said steadily. "You were doing your job as the brother. Josie's fine, and nothing you did would have made a difference with him. You're absolved." In any other setting it would have been a ridiculous thing for a non-priest to say, but Bart whooshed out a breath that sounded suspiciously like a sob, pressed his hands to his eyes, and leaned back against the chair as if all the energy had escaped him.

Josie glanced worriedly toward Tristan for direction. He held up his finger, indicating Bart needed a minute, and they waited in silence until Bart took a new breath, sat up, picked up his sandwich, and took a bite.

The three of them resumed eating as if nothing amiss had happened, and that was the end of that.

CHAPTER 27

"What would you like for supper?" Josie asked. She and Tristan had each worked a full day. Part of her was tired, but part of her still felt the buzz and excitement of working on something new and interesting, actual spy work, innocuous as it had been. Gaines had her highlighting the word "January" on a few court transcripts. She had no idea why he needed that, nor even if it was important, but her imagination told her it was vital. Perhaps even lifesaving. *I'm spy-adjacent, and no one can take that away from me.*

"Let's have dinner with Janine."

Josie swiveled her head to blink at Tristan. "You want to have dinner with my sister. On purpose?"

"Yup," he said, staring doggedly through the windshield.

"She won't come," Josie predicted. "She hates spontaneity. And most restaurants. Possibly also me."

"Only one way to find out," Tristan said, reaching for her phone.

"Wait, how do you know my password?" she asked as he pulled up Janine's number and sent a text.

In return he gave her a little smirk. "I have my ways, Josie Davis."

"Well, that's disturbing," Josie muttered, facing forward again, hands gripping the wheel as she fought heavy DC traffic.

"I'll only use my powers for good where you're concerned," he assured her, resting his hand on her thigh and giving it an affectionate little pat.

"That's only reassuring if I know what your definition of 'good' is. What if you consider stalking good?" she returned.

"Some stalking is good," he said.

"When is stalking ever good?"

"When you're doing it to protect someone," he said.

She waited to look at him again until she stopped at a red light. "Tristan, is this your subtle way of telling me you spied on me while we were apart?"

"Occasionally I checked in, to make certain you were okay."

"How occasionally?" she asked, poking him when he remained silent.

"A lot more than I would care to admit," he said, sighing.

"Tristan," she exclaimed, and the car behind them beeped.

"What?" he asked, genuinely puzzled.

"You don't see the problem here?"

"I sense that you're angry, but I don't know why," he said slowly.

"How would you feel if you found out I'd been secretly spying on you?" she asked.

"That's different."

"Why?"

"Because you would have no reason to spy on me. I was hired to protect you. I needed to check in occasionally, to make sure you were still okay," he said.

"Is that a service you provide to all former clients?" she asked.

"To be fair, you were my first client."

"What about all the ones after?"

"Some cases are still ongoing," he hedged. Her phone beeped and he checked it. "Janine will meet us for supper. Take a right on this street."

She turned right. "Please explain how it is okay for you to stalk me, because I still don't understand."

"First of all, I never stalked. Stalking implies menace. I observed from a distance. It's not like I went through your mail or tried on your shoes while you were out or something."

"What exactly did you do?"

"I did a few drive-bys. Parked and watched your house."

"That was it? You drove by my house a few times?" Her ire turned sheepish because she had done something similar to a couple of exes. Who wasn't guilty of peeping at someone's social media, of listening to gossip to keep tabs? Just because Tristan was silent and hulking didn't make his behavior more disturbing. Did it?

"Turn right here. Mostly."

"Tristan, just tell me."

"I followed you a couple of times."

"When I was alone?"

"A couple of times."

He still stared out his window. Avoiding eye contact?

"And other times?"

"A few times when you were with Eli." He crossed his arms. "Turn left."

"You said you followed me to make certain I was safe, but you had to know I was safe with Eli."

He remained resolute, staring silently out his window with his arms crossed.

"Tristan, you cannot go this silent when we're in the middle of a discussion, especially not when I'm mad at you. It makes me crazy."

"I'm not trying to go silent. I'm keeping an eye on something," he said.

"On what?" she said.

"The person following us. Don't look. Turn right."

"Someone is following us?" she squeaked.

"Yes. Take this left. Speed up by about seven miles per hour. Right. Left. Another left."

She followed his abrupt directions, even weaving in and out of traffic a few times, until he directed her into a multi-level parking garage.

"Take the first open space you see, turn off the car, and duck,"

Tristan said as he took his own advice and reclined his seat. Meanwhile Josie whipped into a space, turned off the car, and ducked low.

They stayed that way, Tristan perfectly silent and still, Josie attempting to control her labored breathing. She had no idea why she was huffing and puffing. It wasn't as if driving had exerted her. Maybe fear made her breathe harder and faster?

"Do you have a mirror?" Tristan whispered after a while.

Josie dug in her purse and handed it to him.

He held it up, angling it all around the car to see around them.

"I think it's safe, but we'll give it a few more minutes before we leave," he said, snapping the mirror closed. She thought he was handing it to her when he put out his hand, but instead he snagged her fingers threading them through his. "I'm sorry."

"Why? They were following me, not you."

"No, I'm sorry for the thing before. You were right. It was wrong of me to follow and spy on you, especially after I'm the one who pushed you away. I just…" He trailed off and blew out a frustrated breath.

"Just what?" she asked, holding her own breath. Would he actually answer?

"Missed you," he croaked, Adam's apple bobbing as his eyes swept her face, hungrily, she thought. If she didn't know better, she might think he couldn't get enough of her.

"Then why…" she began, but cut herself off. She couldn't press him, couldn't force him, couldn't pin him down. That was what made Tristan interesting and appealing and maddening all at once. He was different from other guys she had known and dated, and this was an example of one of those differences: Tristan could not be controlled or contained. Every other guy had been predictable because she knew them so well. Even Gabe. Even though his script often hurt her, he hadn't strayed from it. With Tristan she had no idea what he was going to say or do, and it was as thrilling as it was terrifying. It was possible he might break her heart, but it was also possible he might be the best thing that had ever happened to her. Only time would tell, time and a giant leap off the cliff they were circling.

"Is it the same for you?" Josie said, apropos of nothing for him because he hadn't been privy to her thought processes.

"What?" he said, free hand reaching out to cup her cheek. The thought that he might be as afraid of her as she was of him was even more exciting somehow. She had always been so harmless, so easily dismissed. The fact that Tristan, of all people, might find her breath-taking sent an unexpected jolt of adrenaline and confidence, straight to her brain.

Instead of answering him, she reached out and pressed her free hand to his heart, smiling when it pounded hard beneath her fingers. Whatever he felt for her, it was something, and it was powerful. Maybe she didn't have to have all the answers; maybe it didn't have to be mapped out. Maybe there was no guarantee that he wouldn't destroy her. But wouldn't the possibility that he might not hurt her be worth a leap from anywhere?

"Josie, you have crazy eyes," he whispered, but there was a smile in his voice, if not on his face.

"They match my thoughts right now, as well as my intentions."

"What intentio…" he started, but had to cut off when she kissed him, an all-in possessive sort of kiss he readily returned.

Reluctantly, she drew away, resting her head against the seat, eyes closed.

"What was that for? Not that I'm complaining, but you seemed intent," Tristan said.

"For bravery."

"For you or for me?" he asked.

"Both." She opened her eyes and found him staring at her with his usual intensity.

"Josie," he croaked.

"What?" she said.

"Nothing." He took in a deep breath, held it a few beats, then let it out. "Just *Josie*." He leaned forward and brushed his lips softly to hers, so softly it felt like a tender caress. "I missed your Josieness."

"Tristan," Josie whispered, and he tensed in response to her tone.

"What?"

"I know you're not technically my bodyguard any longer, but can you please do one thing for me?"

"Anything," he said sincerely, still tense. "I would do anything for you."

She took his bigger hand in both hers. "Could you pretty please protect me from my big sister? She terrifies me."

"I'll try," Tristan said, tone turning wry as he relaxed the tense set of his shoulders. "Maybe when this is over Gaines should recruit her."

"You guys have a psychological warfare division?" Josie enquired and she could swear he came so close to losing it that he had to turn and look out his window to avoid letting her see him laugh.

He cleared his throat. "We should go. Being early gives us the advantage."

"I wish we didn't need one so much," Josie said, sounding as melancholy as she felt.

Tristan rested his hand on her thigh, giving it a soothing little squeeze, and they took off.

⚷

They arrived at the restaurant ten minutes early, but Janine still beat them.

"Power play," Tristan muttered. Intent on running interference, he took Josie's hand when she was out of the car, using it to lead her into the restaurant. Josie wondered if there was some sort of alpha male connection that ran from his body to her hormones, because she felt overtly feminine as they walked up the sidewalk and through the dim restaurant—diminutive, girly, and protected. Almost but not quite a little swoony, if she were being honest. Tristan was so *manly,* and she never in a million years thought that quality would be attractive to her. All through school she'd gone out with guys like Gabe and Eli, intelligent, nerdy, quirky guys. She and the meathead athletes had given each other a mutually wide berth. And now here was one, directly in her path, and she suddenly understood the appeal, understood it on a physical level, yes, but on an unexpectedly emotional level that surprised her. Her heart, her very substance, pinged in response to Tristan. She was endlessly fascinated by her response to him, and by his perceived response to her. If someone drew a caricature of her when she looked at him, she was fairly certain she would have heart eyes. And she thought he might have the same when he looked at her.

Of course none of those love-struck expressions dared surface when she was so close to her sister's proximity. Janine sat at the table staring straight ahead with her hands folded, as if she were the mafia don about to decide someone's fate, based on the outcome of the pending meeting. Her gaze fell on Tristan's hand where it was latched onto Josie's and turned into a full grimace of distaste.

"Well, apparently this is back on," was her sour greeting.

"I don't think it was ever off," Tristan said, and brought Josie's fingers to his lips, brushing them with an affectionate kiss as he tossed her a wink.

Danger, full blown swoon in progress. Must hide happiness from sister. Josie tried to come up with something suave, in order to deflect Janine's disapproval, but when she opened her mouth a little squawk came out, like a fledgling sparrow in distress.

Tristan, bizarre person he was, seemed to find it charming.

Janine clucked, as if the sound was further proof of Josie's instability; as if she had ever needed further proof.

"Enjoy it while it lasts," Janine said. "I can tell you for certain it won't last long."

Josie took her cue from Tristan, who ignored the barb and used his good arm to hold Josie's chair, waiting to sit until she had been seated. He reached for the menu and skimmed it while Janine scowled impatiently at the top of his head. "Was there a reason for this impromptu meeting?" she asked at last.

Tristan glanced up with an attempt at innocence, but it was hard to radiate that when you were well over six feet, bulky, and naturally menacing. "Does there have to be a reason to have supper with your little sister?"

That stumped Janine, whose eyes flew to Josie before narrowing.

"You're not married are you? Please tell me you didn't elope. Or, oh, no, are you pregnant? You're pregnant. Mom and Dad are going to flip." She reached for her phone, as if to call their parents and commiserate, and Josie's panicked gaze flew to Tristan for direction.

"I…" she began, not knowing where to go next.

Tristan put up a hand and said, "Whoa," halting both women. Miraculously, it worked to make Janine freeze, hand gripping her phone hard enough to snap it. "If Josie and I were married and/or pregnant, which for the record we are not, why would it be any concern of yours? And why would it be bad news? Josie is a gainfully employed and responsible adult, and so am I." He tipped his head a little, probing Janine's psyche. Her gaze darted away, avoiding him.

"It's not right," Janine murmured.

"What's not right? That Josie should find happiness in the midst of your misery, or that Josie should find happiness at all?"

Janine scowled at him. "Of course I want Josie to be happy, regardless of my own misery. But Josie needs protected."

It was like watching a movie, Josie thought. And though Janine was her big sister, she somehow knew Tristan was the one who had her best interest at heart in this scenario. Watching him pick apart the threads that made up her taciturn older sister was as fascinating as it was scary. Because Josie had the sense she wasn't going to like anything she was about to learn. A part of her wanted to run away and hide from the coming revelation; the other part of her remained rooted to the spot, resigned to hearing the truth and using it to set herself free from the nightmare prison she'd put herself in ten years ago as an eighteen year old kid.

"From what?" Tristan prodded gently.

Janine swallowed hard and used her hand to motion toward Josie. "She's…she's soft and vulnerable and flighty."

Instead of arguing that Josie was none of those things, Tristan turned it around on her. "Aren't you those things?"

Janine shook her head, a little furiously. "No. Not since before I can remember, not since I was a kid."

"Not since Keith," Tristan said, and Josie and Janine both flinched at the name of Janine's ex-husband.

"Leave him out of this," Janine whispered, and now she was the one who looked and sounded afraid.

CHAPTER 28

"I don't think we can," Tristan said after a lengthy and significant pause, one in which Janine's face lost all color and Josie resisted the urge to squirm.

Keith? What did her loathsome former brother-in-law have to do with anything? Apparently something, if Tristan brought him up and Janine reacted the way she had now reacted.

"He has nothing to do with this," Janine insisted.

"You were high school sweethearts, right?" Tristan said, tone softening.

The new tone worked to soften Janine, in response. It was easy to imagine him as a cop, working over suspects. Josie's mind tried to drift to his past, to wonder what went wrong that pulled him out of that life. She redirected it to her sister and the current scenario.

"Yes, we started dating my senior year," Janine said.

The waitress arrived to take their drink order. Tristan waylaid her, putting in their food order, as well. Josie knew it was so their flow wouldn't be interrupted again. After the waitress left, Janine tried to redirect to something else.

"So what *is* going on with you two?" Nervously she sipped her water, hands shaking.

"Everything," Tristan said, and now Janine and Josie stared at him, minds whirring. If Josie thought it was a tactic to distract Janine, that was dispelled when he rested his hand on her leg, giving it a reassuring little squeeze. To her that squeeze seemed to say, *I meant what I said, and we're in this together.*

"Everything," Josie agreed, reaching across him to squeeze *his* leg.

His gaze flicked to her, amused. It was amazing to her now that she could read the amusement in his otherwise stoic features. He didn't smile, but she saw it nonetheless.

"Well, that's fantastic," Janine said, her deadpan tone telling them it was anything but. "I'm so glad life is working out for you."

"Unlike for you," Tristan said, swiveling his head to rest his intent gaze on her. And, like anyone under his direct focus, Janine squirmed.

"I'm doing okay," she said.

He let that lay a few beats. Whether he didn't believe her or didn't care, Josie couldn't be certain. Maybe it wasn't important to the story, in his view. Josie, on the other hand, was glad to hear it. Painful as it was, she suspected that the separation might be a relief in a way. For as long as they had been together, Janine and Keith had had problems. Perhaps it was disloyal of her, but Josie had always chalked those problems up to Janine's difficult personality. But what if Janine wasn't the problem? What if it was Keith?

"Did you meet at school?" Tristan asked.

Janine shook her head. "He's a few years older. I worked as a waitress for the dairy bar. We sold burgers, along with ice cream. Keith was a regular customer. He started matching his appearances to the hours I worked and eventually asked me out."

"Did your parents have a problem with that?" Tristan asked.

Janine shrugged.

Josie had no idea what that meant. She tried to think back to when Janine was in high school. Had dating an older guy bothered their parents? Josie couldn't remember, but she did recall a lot of arguments. Again, she had chalked it up to Janine being Janine. What if there had been a reason?

"He's only three years older," Josie inserted. "That's not so much."

"Not so much," Tristan agreed. "But maybe they had other concerns about him." The question was clearly leading.

Janine shrugged one shoulder. "He was from the wrong side of the tracks, I guess you'd say."

Josie stared at her sister, digesting that. She had been too young to think or know about socio-economic status back then, twelve to Janine's seventeen. Keith had seemed far removed from her and her world and had always remained peripheral, her sister's husband, never her true brother. She felt as if she were hovering at the edge of the same cliff she'd hovered since she met Tristan, one where she would subsequently be forced to re-evaluate everything she'd always assumed as truth.

"When Josie was in high school, she took over the same job you'd once had, working the counter at the dairy bar," Tristan said, apropos of nothing. Or maybe not because Janine flinched and then froze, trying to smooth her reaction.

"Mm, hmm," she said, nodding.

Tristan's eyes bored into her. "That seems like the perfect job for a kid, fairly easy and protected. A safe place for a girl like Josie, who tended to be a bit sensitive and naïve."

Josie frowned at hearing herself described so. Not that she disagreed, but still. Never fun to hear how wide eyed and innocent you were, especially when she'd viewed herself the opposite, mature and sophisticated.

Janine nodded again and began tinkering with a sugar packet, eyes downcast.

"You must have had some sway, to get her your old job," Tristan noted.

Janine nodded again.

"Your husband's cousin owns the dairy bar," Tristan continued.

Josie's brows rose. "Keith's family owns the *Snack Shack*?" she said. If she'd ever heard that before, it didn't register. She wondered how Tristan found out but, knowing Tristan as she did, he would likely search for any pattern or connection. What did it mean that he'd found one?

"They're distantly related," Janine said, now using both hands to roll the sugar packet into a tiny cylinder.

"I looked into their financials," Tristan said.

Janine stilled again, face flushed. "Hmm."

"Janine."

She swallowed hard and finally met his eyes.

"Do you want to tell me, or do you want me to say what I think I know?" Tristan asked.

Janine shook her head.

"What?" Josie prompted. "What do you know?"

"Don't," Janine said, voice breaking as she reached for her napkin and pressed it to wet eyes.

Josie swiveled from the shocking sight of her sister's tears to the stern set of Tristan's features. They remained silent a few beats as their food arrived. Even though Josie was famished, she ignored the food in favor of the more interesting drama unfolding around her. "Tristan, what?" Her heart thundered, sure she was about to hear something that would change her life forever. What she didn't know, what she couldn't guess, was whether the change would be good or bad.

"The *Snack Shack* was a front for drugs and money," Tristan declared.

Josie blinked at him, one half of her sure he must be joking, the other half certain he wasn't. But her certainty came from her trust in him, not what he'd said. "What? I would have noticed that."

He shook his head. "It was a seamless operation. Regular customers came and went, ordering the special. I'm guessing one of the cooks or line preps was the one to prepare the 'order.' You were merely the patsy who handed it over and took the money."

She swallowed hard and looked at Janine who still had her hand pressed to her eyes. "Okay," she said slowly. "That's bad, but I didn't know what I was doing. I can't be held liable, right?"

"No, baby, it's about more than that. Ten years ago, at around the same time this happened, someone was murdered, a local dealer."

"Okay," Josie said, voice shaky with shock and confusion.

"I'm guessing someone put a stop to the little operation at the *Snack Shack,* and there were reparations. Nothing like that comes to a halt without consequences. The murder of the local dealer was eventually solved. This man was arrested and went to prison." He turned his phone to face her, and Josie froze, all the blood draining from her body.

The man from the street, the man who had threatened her, the man from every nightmare the last decade, stared back at her. "It's him," she whispered, breathless with dread.

"I thought so," Tristan said. "He was released from prison a few weeks ago. What I don't know is why he threatened Josie. Maybe Janine can fill in the blanks."

Janine shook her head.

"Janine," Tristan said, tone stern and demanding.

She shook her head again.

"Janine," Josie said, but her tone was filled with hurt, dismay, and confusion.

Janine shuddered and lowered the napkin. "I didn't know, okay? I didn't know at first what was going on, otherwise I never would have gotten you the job." She ended the impassioned little speech with a shuddered sob and this time pressed the napkin to her mouth.

"I'm going to tell you what I think happened, and you tell me if I'm wrong," Tristan said. Janine twisted her napkin between her fingers, tearing it to shreds. "You worked at the *Snack Shack* and met Keith. He told you they needed you to do something, no big deal, hand over a paper sack, take the money. It wasn't so far outside of what you were already doing."

"I didn't know at first what it was," Janine interjected. "I didn't figure it out until later, until after we'd been together for a while." She sounded plaintive and miserable.

"When Josie got the job, you thought she'd be safe. Obviously Keith would never involve your innocent little sister in his scheme."

"Josie could never keep a secret, she has no poker face," Janine whispered, darting a glance toward Josie and away again with a little shudder.

"But if Josie didn't know it was going on, it was the perfect setup. Who would ever believe such a cherub would pass drugs and laundered money?" Tristan mused.

Janine shook her head and started to rock back and forth in her chair.

"You found out, though," Tristan said.

"I overheard Keith and his cousin laughing about it," Janine whispered.

"You put your foot down," Tristan guessed.

For the first time, Janine's eyes flashed with some of her former spirit. "Of course I did. I didn't want them to use my little sister that way. It was dangerous and wrong. I was furious. That was the first time I left Keith."

"Then what happened?" Tristan said. Josie didn't think it was an accident that he softened his tone. This must be the part of the story he didn't know, couldn't guess.

Janine took a shaky breath. "Keith said it was out of his hands, that he was just the messenger and had nothing to do with it. I chose to believe him, so I went over his head, to his cousin. I told him he couldn't use Josie that way."

"What was his reaction to that?" Tristan asked.

"He laughed, said it was too late, Josie was the perfect patsy because she had no idea what was going on and no one would ever suspect her. I said it was too dangerous and I wanted her out." She paused and pressed her lips together.

"And then?" Tristan prompted.

"And then I left and made an anonymous tip to the police about all the drugs. They were in the middle of setting up a sting when it all fell apart. Keith's cousin got wind of the sting and the guy got killed… and…and something got lost in translation, I don't know. The guy, the higher up guy, the one who killed the drug runner, thought Josie was the one who found out about everything and busted them." Again her glance flicked to Josie and away.

"That was when he threatened Josie."

Janine swallowed hard and nodded. "But then he got arrested, he went to prison. It was over. It was all *over*."

"It wasn't over, though," Josie whispered. "For me, it only started. I was terrified, and no one believed me. Everyone thought I made it up, Mom and Dad, the police, everyone. But you *knew*. You knew it was real, that it happened, and you did nothing, said nothing."

"I did *everything*," Janine argued. "I lost my marriage because I went to bat for you."

Josie blinked at her vehement tone. Some of Janine's resentment began to make sense, at least from her point of view. "I didn't do anything," Josie argued. "I didn't even know this went on. You have blamed me for things I couldn't possibly control. And on top of that you gaslighted me into believing I was a drama queen for being afraid, of a very real threat. How could you keep this secret from me for ten years?"

"Because I had everything to lose," Janine exclaimed, so loudly that several people darted her a look. "On top of my marriage, there was the very real issue of my involvement, along with Keith's. He could have gone to prison, Josie. *I* could have gone to prison."

Josie didn't reply. She merely stared at her sister, wondering how she could ever overcome what felt like a decade of betrayal. Janine had let her linger in terror, in order to save herself and her husband.

"I put everything on the line for you. I put my *life* on the line for you, to get you out of that situation and save you so you wouldn't get sucked under. Don't put this on me because you had to be afraid. Your fear doesn't hold a candle to mine," Janine said. As if to prove her fear, her hands shook and her lips trembled.

Still Josie didn't reply. She merely stared at her sister, wondering if she'd ever actually known her. Janine flinched as if Josie had slapped her.

"Please don't tell Mom and Dad and Bart," she pleaded, wringing her hands together in misery.

"Josie will tell whoever she wants, whatever she wants," Tristan interjected. "She's done living in the shadow of secrets, yours or anyone else's."

Josie still had no words, but she tore her gaze off Janine and onto him. He stared down at her with blazing intensity that reassured her. Tristan was a rock, *her* rock. He had stepped into her life and wrenched her into the light of truth, even truth she hadn't wanted to face. And it wasn't an exaggeration to say that truth had set her free. No longer was she terrified. No longer did she question her sanity, her very worth. The problem wasn't with her, had never been with her. It was with her family, who had tried so hard to shield her from reality that they had instead put her in a gilded cage of their making. No more. She would face the hard realities of life, even if they broke her. But somehow she knew they wouldn't. She was strong and resilient, and she would be for the rest of her life.

"I love you," she blurted.

Tristan's expression didn't change, but his eyes widened, and then the chair across from them clattered to the ground as Janine made her escape.

CHAPTER 29

Tristan sighed. "Of course she's a runner. Come on." He tossed some bills onto the table and stood, taking Josie's hand to lead her out of the restaurant. People stared as they made their escape, no doubt wondering what was up and why they'd been such a spectacle. Josie couldn't care, mostly because she felt void of anything except shock. For ten years her sister had not only lied, she had blatantly made light of Josie's deep fear, intimating instead that Josie made everything up. Suddenly Tristan felt like the only real thing in her life, and she was intensely thankful that he held her hand as he directed her out of the restaurant and into the suddenly blazing sunlight that blinded them.

Nearby, a car started. Squinting, Tristan pulled his sunglasses out of his shirtfront and put them on, but before he could do so Josie realized the awful truth and froze in horror. The car was headed straight for them, seemed intent on hitting them and pinning them to the wall like butterflies on exhibit. Worse, they were hemmed in, there was nowhere to run. Tristan seemed to realize the same thing, his eyes darting frantically as his hand gripped Josie's. She understood that grip, it was the kind that meant he was about to toss her away, to offer himself as sacrifice to save her. But there was no way she would allow it. She hugged him, both arms cinching around him like a koala. He couldn't try to put her behind him and take the brunt; they would go together.

"Josie, no," he shouted, attempting to use his hands to pry her away. If both of them had been fully functioning, he might have succeeded. As it was, one arm lacked all strength, meaning he couldn't push Josie off him, like he wanted.

Josie closed her eyes, bracing for an impact that never arrived. She couldn't understand. Her body was tensed and alert, ready to be smashed. The sound arrived, metal on metal, a horrible crash, but no pain. Was she dead? Had her spine snapped?

She chanced opening her eyes and realized Tristan stared straight ahead, mouth open in shock, the most reaction she had ever seen from him.

Following the line of his gaze, she saw two cars mangled together, the first mystery vehicle and, *"Janine,"* she yelled, letting go of Tristan to try and reach her sister, the same sister who had used her car as a battering ram to save Josie.

Tristan, hot on her heels, soon overtook her and wrenched open the door, crouching next to Janine, now bent over her wheel and bleeding.

"Janine," Josie repeated as Tristan shifted into first responder mode, checking Janine's pulse, pupils, neck, and bones while simultaneously grasping his phone and calling 911. "Oh, Janine."

Janine was still. Blood poured from her head but, to Josie's extreme relief, she blinked. "I only ever wanted to save you," she said weakly to Josie.

"I know," Josie said, which was a half lie. It would probably take a long time to parse through the last decade of sisterly turmoil. Janine was complicated, and so were her motivations and actions. But the truth was that she *had* saved Josie, both when she was eighteen and now. And, as much as she still had hurt feelings over everything, Josie owed her for that. "You're going to be okay," she said, but her tone was a question as she turned to Tristan and got his opinion on the matter.

"Vitals look good, some head trauma, but no obvious breaks that I can tell. Sit still and wait for the medics to move you, they'll assess for internal damage." He stood upright and squeezed Josie's shoulder with his good hand. "I need to check on that guy." Then he withdrew his gun and walked to the other car.

As much as Josie wanted to be present for her sister, she also needed to see and know who was in the other car. Not too far away, she could hear the first sirens approach. Janine was becoming more alert, a good sign, as far as Josie could tell. "I'll be back in a second," she told her sister, and went to stand beside Tristan.

Together, they surveyed the person in the car beside them. Tristan had lowered his weapon to his side and tucked it away when Josie joined him. When she reached him she saw why. Her tormenter, the man who had changed the trajectory of her life a decade ago—turning her from a sheltered and happy-go-lucky eighteen year old into a terrified, paranoid wreck—lay dead and unseeing, blood oozing from his nose and ears.

"Oh," Josie said, uncertain how she felt over the sight of him. Relieved? Not really. She had already found relief and an end to her fear through Tristan. Sad? Not that, either. Mostly she felt disturbed at the loss of life, at all the tragedy that had stemmed from so many poor decisions. And something else, maybe later she would call it closure. Whatever it was, she had seen enough and returned promptly to Janine's side.

"I'm probably going to go to jail," Janine murmured. "And maybe I deserve it."

"You're not going to go to jail for this; you saved us. Tristan will tell them," Josie assured her.

"What about the other stuff? The drugs." She closed her eyes. "I can't even believe I'm saying that. Me, and drugs. Everything got so messed up, Josie. I loved Keith, and I was so desperate to be with him, to stay together. I've never been as strong as you are, as okay with being alone."

Josie's lashes fluttered. Her sister thought she was strong? That she was okay with being alone? In retrospect, Janine had gone straight from her parents' home to Keith's. Josie had been on her own since she graduated college six years ago. Perspective was the strongest drug, stronger than reality, apparently. "You will find the strength to do whatever you need to do, I know you will. And we'll be with you."

"I'm sorry," Janine muttered, closing her eyes. "Really sorry."

"It's okay," Josie said, swallowing past a hard lump. She wasn't certain she meant it, but she was certain she would someday. The ambulance arrived at the same time as the police. They, of course, began talking to Tristan who, even in civilian clothes, practically screamed "I AM LAW ENFORCEMENT ADJACENT." The medics unloaded and gently bumped Josie aside while they tended to Janine. She couldn't see what they were doing, so she focused on Tristan, who now stood with his feet firmly planted, uninjured hand tucked behind his back, the classic, I'm-the-alpha-male-in-charge pose. Where did he come from? And why? The temptation to Google him was almost too much, but she had promised she wouldn't. She sighed, realizing that if they had any chance, she would have to trust him and be trustworthy in return.

Soon the medics had Janine loaded.

"You coming?" One of them asked Josie.

Josie glanced at Tristan, still deeply involved in conversation. She had made the last move when she blurted her feelings for him. The ball was in his court now, all she could do was give him the space to toss it back. "I'm coming," she said and followed the medic to the waiting ambulance.

As she sat in the ambulance, she texted her parents and Bart, giving them the abridged version, that Janine was in an accident and on her way to the hospital. They arrived at the ER and Josie was allowed to stay with Janine while she was triaged. Everything looked good on arrival, especially her vitals, but they wanted to send her for an MRI to check for any internal damage to her organs.

They came to retrieve her, and Josie headed to the waiting room to greet her family.

"Josie," her mom said, dodging to her feet to offer up a hug. "What on earth happened?"

"I..." Josie began and didn't know how to continue. Wearily, she sank into a chair. "It's a really long story, Mom. I promise to tell you later, but for now can we not talk? I haven't eaten in hours, and I'm exhausted and in shock and about ten other things."

Bart sank into the seat beside her. "I'll get you some food, kiddo. Anything sound good?"

Tristan, Josie thought, heart pinging. Instead she smiled at her brother. "A burger or something would be awesome, thank you. Our meal was interrupted, and we didn't get to eat."

"Sure," Bart said, giving her leg a pat. He stood and ambled toward the cafeteria.

"I'll go with him," her dad said. He was clearly antsy and in need of something to take his focus.

"I don't understand how this happened," her mom mused. "On top of the divorce and everything. It seems like everything bad happens to Janine." She let out a long breath.

Josie rested her head on her shoulder. "Janine will be okay; we'll all be okay."

"Don't tell your sister, but we never liked Keith," her mom said.

Probably with good reason, Josie thought. Someday they would all have to clear the air about everything. Tristan was right, secrets were no good and Josie was done with them. However, she also realized there was a time and a place. Right now, in this emergency room, was not the time or place. Her phone beeped with a text. She gave it a hopeful glance, but it wasn't Tristan.

"Who's that?" her mom nosily asked.

"Eli," Josie said before reading his text to herself. *Hey. Haven't heard from you in a few days. You okay?*

She blew out a breath. Where to begin? *Janine's been in an accident. I'm actually at the ER now.*

Geez, Eli replied, which made her laugh because she could hear it in his voice. And then she felt sad. She liked Eli, had always liked Eli. He had been a good and fun friend and she desperately hoped she hadn't hurt him. *Want some company?*

Did she? Was it taking advantage of their friendship if she asked him to come? On the other hand, they probably needed to have a conversation. *Yes.*

Fifteen minutes later, Eli arrived and greeted her family. Josie had already eaten her burger, and she felt better with the advent of higher blood sugar. Eli finished the hellos to her family and raised his brows at Josie. "Want to take a walk with me? I saw a green line back there, just dying to be explored."

She laughed, which was her usual reaction to Eli. "I'd love to."

"What's up with Janine?" he asked as they left the ER.

"She's banged up, and might have a concussion, but she should be okay. Mom's with her now, so I'm safe to wander."

"Safe for who? Because you're lethal, Josie," Eli said, but his tone sounded a little melancholy.

Josie sighed.

Eli laughed. "Just spit it out, woman."

"I'm sorry," Josie said in an impassioned tone as she reached for his hand and gave it a squeeze.

"Why are you sorry?" He let go of her hand and put his arm around her shoulders. "Josie, we've been pals a long time. I always thought you were cute and funny, in a weird quirky girl sort of way. But I steered clear because of Gabe. And then when it became clear that you realized Gabe is a…"

"Putz?" Josie supplied.

"Of the highest order," Eli agreed. "And then Tristan was out of the picture, I thought maybe you and I…" He trailed away. "We have fun together."

"So much fun."

"On paper we're a good match."

"Such a good match," she agreed.

"But that doesn't mean we're in love. We've had some fun, nothing that's advanced past our long and nice friendship. Did I maybe hope it might turn into something more? Kind of. Am I heartbroken that it won't? Kind of, but that's on me, not on you. You have never promised me more than what you've already given, and we are okay. More than.

We're friends, the same friends we've always been." He gave her shoulders another encouraging squeeze.

"Eli, you are the best, and I love you to pieces," Josie said, using both arms to give him a hard squeeze. He tipped his head, resting it on hers, and that was the exact moment Tristan poked his head around the corner behind them and observed the exchange.

CHAPTER 30

Two weeks later, Josie's phone had become the enemy. Its silence beckoned her, encouraging her to call, to text, to Google, to stalk. She did none of those things and, when the inducement grew too great, shoved her phone into a drawer where she couldn't see it and be lured by it. She was proud of the fact that she refused to give in to her temptation. On the other hand, she was dismayed by how much Tristan's silence hurt. Had he gone away forever? Did he feel nothing for her?

She tried to go on as if everything was normal that day, even attending Eli's cousin's wedding with him. Though she had technically been his date, nothing romantic had happened between them. Eli was the same funny pal he'd always been. Josie was both relieved and grateful and tried hard to pay attention to him and only him that day, making certain to make a good impression on his family. But since then she'd stumbled under the apprehension that Tristan was gone, possibly forever this time.

And then, exactly fourteen days after Janine's accident, he knocked on her door. She opened it and blinked at him in shock, lashes fluttering with uncertainty. "Are you a hallucination?"

"If anyone is a dream in this scenario, it's you," he said, fingers reaching out to touch the sleeve of her soft sweater. "It's July. Why are you wearing a sweater?"

"I get cold in the house," she said.

"Why not turn down the air?"

"Don't mess with my system," she told him.

They regarded each other in silence.

"Can I come in?" he asked.

"That depends," she said.

"On what?" he asked.

"On whether you're about to pop into my life, only to painfully disappear again."

"I wanted to…" his eyes flicked to the ground and then back to hers. "Talk. After that, I think you're going to have to be the one to decide if you want me to disappear."

She opened the door and stepped aside, granting him access. He took a step inside, closed his eyes, and took a deep breath, letting it out as her name. "*Josie.*"

"Would you like coffee or tea or mushrooms?"

"Mushrooms?" he asked, eyes opening wide.

"I was chopping mushrooms for something, and it was all that came to mind at first. But I also have cookies, if you'd prefer."

"Who would prefer cookies to mushrooms?" Tristan asked and he was doing the thing again, the one that made him sound amused, despite no visual change in his demeanor.

"We could pair the two, if you'd like," she offered.

"I'm good with only conversation, if that's all right."

"Okay," she said, wishing he had asked for something to eat or drink. She needed something to do with her hands. Without purpose, they fluttered nervously and clasped together in front of her, making her stride awkward and stilted. She led him to the living room and sat on the couch. He sat beside her, on the next cushion, leaving the space on his other side available. It was a purposeful placement, the lack of space between them when there was so much to choose from. He took a deep breath.

"I told you my family's not great."

"Oh, you're starting, just like that?"

"Do you need a preamble? Like four score and eighteen years ago?"

"I thought you might need that," she said.

"What I need…" he began. His hand reached out toward her and hovered, not making contact, until he dropped it and took a steadying breath.

"Your family wasn't great," Josie prompted, when it became apparent he'd lost his focus.

"Right. Not great is probably the best way to phrase it for now. I went to school and was pretty much a candidate for failure. I had no support system, lots of chaos, hated sitting still, being quiet, all the things school wants you to be. But I had this teacher." He paused and it was ridiculous how jealous Josie felt over the softness now in his features and tone.

"She was pretty?" Josie guessed.

"She was *old*," Tristan said wryly. "But she was gentle and kind and nurturing and basically everything I'd never had before, never known existed before. It was like being buffed with a big, fluffy towel all the time. Her name was Mrs. Connelly, and I thought she was perfect. Crazy enough, she seemed to think I was pretty great, too. She started me on a different trajectory, one that did pretty well in school, one that enjoyed learning, however much I kept that fact to myself. Don't get me wrong, I wasn't an honors kid. But I passed, I did all right, I kept my nose clean. And it was all because of Mrs. Connelly, because my first taste of school was good, was great. I said all this as a preface, so you'd understand what's about to come next because," he paused and huffed a breath, gearing up, "See, Josie, I'm not a relationship guy. It was kind of a joke, among people who knew me, that I don't settle down, that I don't *want* to settle down, maybe can't settle down. But, Josie, I swear to you that the moment I walked into your classroom that first day, everything changed. I saw you sitting on the floor sorting crayons in your little cardigan and…" He broke off and shook his head, searching for words that seemed to be trying to escape him. "It was less like a lightning bolt to the heart, and more like coming home. Because in all my life, you are only the second person who has made me feel like I can be more than what I am, that I *want* to be more, and all these months have been exactly that, *so much wanting.*"

He paused and stared at her, his eyes doing the intense sweep of her they always did, only now she had a name for it: want. And his breath hitched in a way it never had, becoming ragged on the intake, as if it hurt to finally tell her these things, to reveal himself and be vulnerable in this way. Josie knew that for a guy like him, who could take a bullet and keep going, this was perhaps the scariest thing he had ever done. She eased a tiny bit closer and tipped her head, encouraging him to continue.

He remained exactly as he was, stony and still, a few inches separating them. So it was up to Josie to bridge the gap and touch him. Her fingers eked out, crawling tentatively to him like a little spider, coming to rest on his thigh. She gave it a little tap. "Then why? Tell me," she demanded gently, because it seemed like he needed gentleness, or was about to.

He picked up her fingers and held them tenderly in his much bigger hand. "You know I was a cop."

She nodded.

"It wasn't easy being a cop, not from a family like mine, not from a neighborhood like mine. A lot of people from my circle went the opposite direction, but I always wanted to help, to make the world better." He puffed a breath of air and shook his head. "What a joke."

She gave his fingers an encouraging squeeze.

"Let me preface by saying that I grew up in St. Louis, downtown. In my high school, being white meant I was in the minority, and I loved it. Most of my best friends were black. To me that was normal. Race genuinely wasn't something that mattered to me, or even occurred to me. Most of my teammates from football were black, most of the other cops I counted as coworkers were black. It was what it was." He shrugged. "And then this incident occurred, you probably saw it on the news. A cop killed a kid."

Her brows rose. "That was you?"

He shook his head. "Different shift, but I knew the guy, had worked with him a few years. He was one of the good ones, you know? Good attitude, good ethic, solid and dependable. Not every cop is good, but this guy was. He was gutted about killing that kid, but the kid pulled a knife on him, what was he to do? He has a family. Was he supposed to take the chance of not coming home so the optics would look good?" He blew out a frustrated breath. "Anyway, it set off a powder keg. There were riots. In my circle, it caused a breach because I took the cop's side. Everyone else I knew took the kid's side. And then I was called out to one of the riots. The mayor didn't want the optics to look bad, didn't want it to seem like there was brutality or that we were a police state. The end result of that was that we were badly outnumbered. Probably twenty or thirty to one. Angry mobs are unpredictable and scary at the best of times, but when they're foaming with anger…"

"You were in danger," Josie guessed.

He swallowed hard. "I thought I was going to die that night. We circled each other and tried to hold them off, and it became an all out scrum. We were losing, badly. We had been told not to shoot, no matter what. One of my buddies on the force got knocked to the ground. They pounced on him; he was being trampled, screaming for help, pleading. I took out my stick, and I started swinging, making a path to him, trying to save him."

He paused, staring into space with a grim expression.

Josie squeezed his hand again.

He took a breath, maybe his first in too long. His body and face were tense, and his hand gripped hers painfully now. "Of course the media were there, cameras in our faces, trying to capture every second of the drama. They caught me right as my stick connected with someone, a woman. They didn't capture the part where she hit me and spit in my face. They didn't capture the part where my buddy on the ground started to cry and tell me to tell his wife he loved her. They didn't capture how badly we were outnumbered. All they captured was my stick clipping her head. It made a splashy headline, and I became the face of police brutality."

"That's not fair," Josie interjected hotly. Tristan was the opposite of brutal, was instead careful and gentle in the way big men sometimes are, as if cognizant of their size and ability to inflict damage on those who are smaller.

"There is no fair," Tristan said evenly, tiredly. "I was scapegoated, put on leave, and eventually fired. My former friends and family were all too gleeful at the turn of events. I-told-you-so had never been so painful before. My life became dust: no job, no friends, no future. No department would touch me. I saw Gaines's ad and jumped at it. To me it seemed like a second chance and also a lateral move, I could be peripheral to law enforcement with none of the politics. Gaines knows, of course, is privy to the whole thing. As long as I keep my nose clean here, he doesn't care about before."

He rested his head on the back of the couch. She had never seen him so exhausted before. She thought he had been keeping his emotions at bay, but it turned out he had been holding them too close. Now that he'd let them out, he was drained. He stared at her with sad eyes that gutted her for their hollow emptiness.

She let the silence linger a while, digesting all the new information, searching for the proper words. "That's why you pushed me away?" she said at last.

"Josie, weren't you paying attention? I'm so toxic not even my family wants me. I have no idea how to do this, none. What I told you from the beginning is true: I'm a bad bet on every front."

She studied him, framing her reply. "You are not easy, but when did easy become a synonym for good or worthwhile? It didn't. You were lucky to have your Mrs. Connelly, who saw the potential in you and worked to help you find it. She had her blinders off, saw the real you, and worked to bring that person out. Do you understand that *you* are my first Mrs. Connelly?"

He blinked once and, for him, that was as much of a shocked reaction as he gave. "What?" he rasped.

"My entire life, I have been in a tiny little bottle of other people's expectations, of their lies and inability to deal with my emotions. Everyone made me feel like I was either too much or not enough. And then you happened." She gazed at him in wonder, because that was how she felt. To her, he was a miracle, someone strong enough and brave enough to break her out of the box she'd been living in, to give her fresh eyes, to make her view her life through a different lens, one she never expected to see, one where she could be brave, strong, and daring. He stared at her, as if unable to comprehend.

She eased closer, giving his shoulders an impassioned little shake, for all the good it did. He remained intransient, an immovable wall of muscle. "Tristan, I believed *my* family's lies for far too long. Maybe it's time you stopped believing yours. Their issues are their issues, and they have nothing to do with you. I'm sorry, so sorry, that you got caught up in a false narrative, that you were made the fall guy for someone's political aspirations, for a country's illogical obsession with victimhood. But that has nothing to do with who you are, either."

"Then who am I?" he whispered, with the first hint of vulnerability she'd ever heard from him.

"You are the most intelligent and capable man I've ever met. You're endlessly fascinating, with your stoic work ethic and unwavering discipline. Even after being put through the political wringer in a public forum, your sense of justice has remained intact, and so has your desire to help, protect, and serve. You're singed but not burned, weary but not burned out. You fight for the little guy, stand up for people who can't stand up for themselves, protect the people you care about, and battle for what's right. You are a honey badger when you're on the trail of righting a wrong, you are a throwback to a time gone by, the last remaining dregs of what makes men great. In short, you are a hero."

He blinked at her again, this time in triplicate. "You see all that when you look at me?"

She nodded. "And so much more. *So much.* Because we haven't even touched all that gooey softness that's trapped inside you." Her hand pressed against his heart. "You are brimming with potential, Tristan Evans."

She could see the way her words filled him up. It was what every teacher hoped for, to make a difference in her pupil. Tristan wasn't her pupil, but he was allowing her words to make a difference, to *heal.*

"Josie," he breathed in that way he had, of saying her name like it was oxygen. He put out a hand, resting on her waist. Did it tremble, or was that her overheated imagination? "I have tried to suppress every thought, every feeling, every desire for you since the moment we met. I have lost in the best and most dramatic way possible. There is not one tiny thing about you that I do not adore. You are nothing I ever imagined, and everything I could ever need in my life. Even the way you drive is cute, despite how high the likelihood that it will end in my demise. I arrived in DC crushed, rejected, destroyed, this broken shell of a person. I thought my life was over, but you have singlehand-edly shown me it's not. You have been my spark of light in an under-ground tunnel. Walking into your classroom all those months ago was the greatest moment of my life, the best thing that has ever happened to me." And then he did the unprecedented, he smiled, so big and so deep that his eyes crinkled and Josie counted all of his teeth. And she saw it, the thing he'd been hiding for so long: Tristan had a *dimple*.

"You smiled," she breathed, touching her finger to the divot in his cheek.

"This is how I feel all the time when I'm with you, on the inside," he said, placing his other hand on the other side of her waist. He reeled her closer, until she was pressed against him, and then one of his hands went to her hair, letting the silky tresses flow through his fingers. He sighed like someone who had set down a heavy weight. Josie's hands smoothed over his shoulders, still not used to the impressive bulk there.

"Why did you disappear for two weeks after I told you I loved you?"

"I didn't. I went to the hospital and saw you canoodling with Eli. It looked like, well, I don't have to tell you what it looked like. But then I spent some time following you around and realized it was nothing, that I was mistaken."

Annoyed now, she clutched his lapels and gave them a little shake. "Stop stalking me."

"Stalking implies menace," he reminded her.

"Then what do you call what you've been doing?"

"Hopeful obsession," he replied.

"Stop hopefully obsessing."

"I don't think I can," he said, brushing his lips on hers. He closed his eyes and rested his forehead against hers. "Josie."

"What?"

"This thing hanging over me, the loss of my old life, the start of a new one, it's not an automatic new beginning. It feels like there are all these tethers, weighing me down. So many fissures and cracks that might never heal."

She took his vulnerability for the gift it was, gathering his big hands in her smaller ones. "The Japanese have an art form called *kintsugi*. When a piece of pottery cracks, they don't throw it out. They fill the cracks with gold, to highlight the beauty in the breaks. Everyone has broken pieces, Tristan. I promise I will be gentle and patient and tender with yours. I promise I will try to fill all your broken pieces with gold."

He swallowed hard as he stared at their joined hands, Adam's apple bobbing. "I might break your heart."

"You might," she agreed, nodding. "I don't think you will. But if you do, you won't break *me*. After living the last ten years of my life hiding in the shadows, I'm going to be okay, and you're the one who showed me that and made me believe it. We'll be like ferns, unfurling into this new love together, a little bit at a time, stretching all of our fronds toward the sunlight." She kissed his hands.

He smoothed his thumb over her bottom lip, staring at it. "You make me believe I can be a person who loves you as well as you deserve to be loved."

"You make me believe I can be brave enough to lead the kind of adventurous life you need," she returned.

"Adventure? Josie, I've been in car chases, riots, gang wars, murder investigations, shootings, stabbings, fights, dove into the ocean from a cliff, jumped out of an airplane, swam into an underground cave, won a high school football championship, got shot, and do you know what the greatest moment of all those things was?"

She shook her head.

"It was when I woke up in the hospital and saw you standing at the foot of my bed. I don't want or need adventure; I want your lozenges and your hugs and your cozy yellow kitchen and your fuzzy cardigans and your perfectly sorted crayons in the middle of total chaos. I want peace and rest and softness; I want you, every bit of you, forever. That's all." He tipped her face and kissed her in that way he had, the one that took total control and left her weak and shaky, uncertain if it was day or night or tomorrow or two years from now.

"Now we have a problem," she managed to say when the kiss was finished.

"What's that?" he asked, eyes closed, breathing unsteady.

"Now that I've had a taste, I need some adventure," she said.

He opened his eyes and regarded her. "We have a few weeks left in your summer vacation. What did you have in mind? Name it, and I'll make it happen," he promised. "Do you want to go scuba diving? Shooting range? Parachuting? What does my Josie want?"

"What if, and hear me out, we went on a picnic to the park and…" she gripped his shirt, cinching him dramatically closer as she made her proclamation. "Fed the ducks."

He blinked, waiting for more. "And then…"

"That's it. I want to go to the park and feed the ducks."

"Why is that an adventure?" he asked.

"Have you ever tried to feed the ducks at the park when the big scary geese chase you around, honking and hissing? It's terrifying." She shuddered.

He coughed. She fed him a lozenge on instinct now, a Pavlovian response. He cleared his throat and held up a finger for a few beats before he could speak. "I will take you to the park and protect you from all the scary geese while you feed the ducks." His tone was properly grave.

"Do you promise?" she said.

"I swear it," he said, but he could no longer maintain his solemn visage, and when he finally cracked and started to laugh, Josie thought it was the best gift she had ever been given, at least until he made good on his promise to save her from the scary geese, then and always.

*T*hank you for reading *Chalked and Loaded,* the first book in the Private Spies series. For more books, please check my website at www.vanessagraybartal.com .